Abandoned, alone...and pregnant...

Single mom-to-be Emma Bowen had nowhere to go but back to her hometown of Saddle Falls. There, she would run her late dad's diner and single-handedly create a loving life for her baby. But she'd never rely on a man again. Not even her childhood friend, attorney Josh Ryan, whose protective streak proved broader than his mouthwateringly muscular chest....

She needed his TLC....

Despite Emma's declaration of independence, the pregnant beauty evoked Josh's every masculine instinct—to protect, defend...possess? Whoa! Woman-wary Josh couldn't let Emma and her unborn tyke arouse such wild, sweet longings. Then again, how could he ever relinquish this little family-to-be?

* * *

Don't miss
A Family To Come Home To (SE #1468)
coming next month in Special Edition!

Dear Reader,

Have you started your spring cleaning yet? If not, we have a great motivational plan: For each chore you complete, reward yourself with one Silhouette Romance title! And with the standout selection we have this month, you'll be finished reorganizing closets, steaming carpets and cleaning behind the refrigerator in record time!

Take a much-deserved break with the exciting new ROYALLY WED: THE MISSING HEIR title, *In Pursuit of a Princess,* by Donna Clayton. The search for the missing St. Michel heir leads an undercover princess straight into the arms of a charming prince. Then escape with Diane Pershing's SOULMATES addition, *Cassie's Cowboy*. Could the dreamy hero from her daughter's bedtime stories be for real?

Lugged out and wiped down the patio furniture? Then you deserve a double treat with Cara Colter's *What Child Is This?* and Belinda Barnes's *Daddy's Double Due Date*. In Colter's tender tearjerker, a tiny stranger reunites a couple torn apart by tragedy. And in Barnes's warm romance, a bachelor who isn't the "cootchie-coo" type discovers he's about to have twins!

You're almost there! Once you've rounded up every last dust bunny, you're really going to need some fun. In Terry Essig's *Before You Get to Baby...* and Sharon De Vita's *A Family To Be,* childhood friends discover that love was always right next door. De Vita's series, SADDLE FALLS, moves back to Special Edition next month.

Even if you skip the spring cleaning this year, we hope you don't miss our books. We promise, this is one project you'll love doing.

Happy reading!

Mary-Theresa Hussey

Mary-Theresa Hussey
Senior Editor

A Family To Be

SHARON DE VITA

Published by Silhouette Books

America's Publisher of Contemporary Romance

This one's for the Fabulous Cushing Men—all four of them—for making me feel so welcome, so accepted and so…fortunate to have all of you in my life. Not every woman is lucky enough to gain three brothers along with a husband, but I did. For Michael—may your life always continue to be an adventure; for Bruce—for wonderfully filling in the gap the loss of my own brother left so many years ago; for the late Doug—for the beauty and dignity of your life and your legacy. Oh, yeah, and for my husband, the one and only Colonel—for showing me that life can be beautiful again. Love you guys, The Goober Queen

SILHOUETTE BOOKS

ISBN 0-373-19586-9

A FAMILY TO BE

This edition published by arrangement with Harlequin Books S.A.

Visit Silhouette at www.eHarlequin.com

Printed in U.S.A.

Books by Sharon De Vita

Silhouette Romance

Heavenly Match #475
Lady and the Legend #498
Kane and Mabel #545
Baby Makes Three #573
Sherlock's Home #593
Italian Knights #610
Sweet Adeline #693
***On Baby Patrol* #1276
***Baby with a Badge* #1298
***Baby and the Officer* #1316
††*The Marriage Badge* #1443
†*Anything for Her Family* #1580
†*A Family To Be* #1586

Silhouette Special Edition

Child of Midnight #1013
**The Lone Ranger* #1078
**The Lady and the Sheriff* #1103
**All It Takes Is Family* #1126
††*The Marriage Basket* #1307
††*The Marriage Promise* #1313
†*With Family in Mind* #1450

Silhouette Books

The Coltons
I Married a Sheik

**Lullabies and Love
††The Blackwell Brothers
†Saddle Falls
*Silver Creek County

SHARON DE VITA,

a former adjunct professor of literature and communications, is a *USA Today* bestselling, award-winning author of numerous works of fiction and nonfiction. Her first novel won a national writing competition for Best Unpublished Romance Novel of 1985. This award-winning book, *Heavenly Match,* was subsequently published by Silhouette in 1985. Sharon has over two million copies of her novels in print; her professional credentials have earned her a place in *Who's Who in American Authors, Editors and Poets* as well as in the *International Who's Who of Authors.* In 1987 Sharon was the proud recipient of the *Romantic Times* Lifetime Achievement Award for Excellence in Writing.

A newlywed, Sharon met her husband while doing research for one of her books. The widowed, recently retired military officer was so wonderful, Sharon decided to marry him after she interviewed him! Sharon and her new husband have seven grown children, five grandchildren, and currently reside in Arizona.

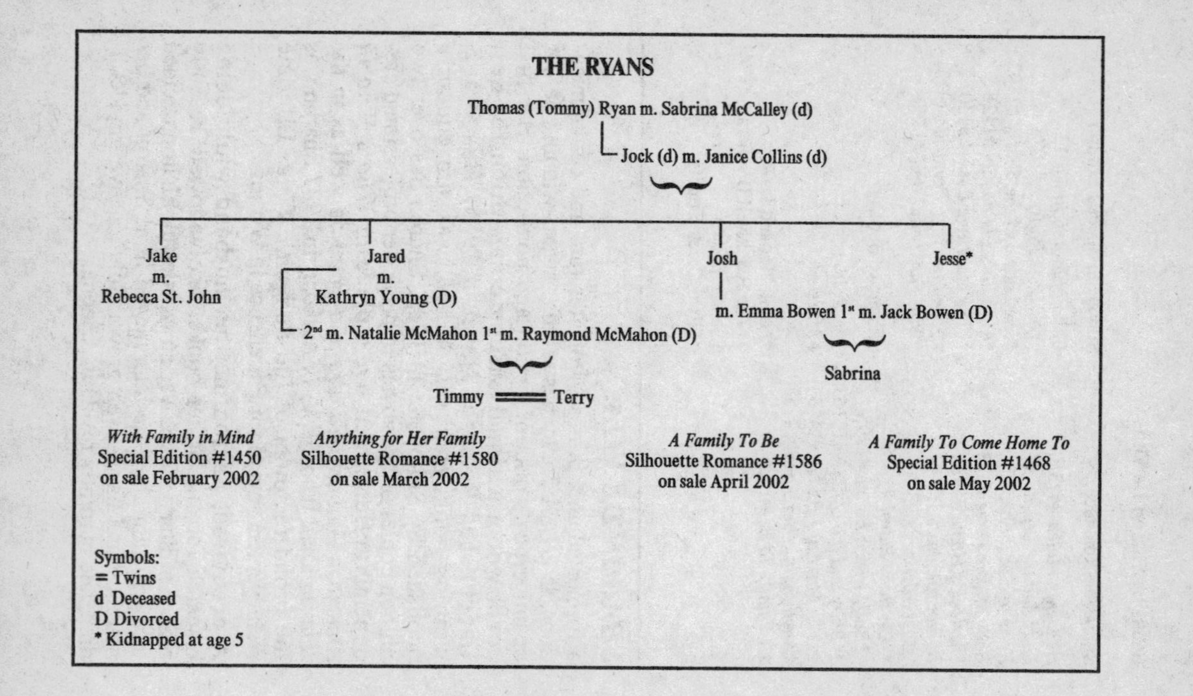
THE RYANS
Thomas (Tommy) Ryan m. Sabrina McCalley (d)
Jock (d) m. Janice Collins (d)
Jake
m.
Rebecca St. John
Jared
m.
Kathryn Young (D)
2nd m. Natalie McMahon 1st m. Raymond McMahon (D)
Timmy = Terry
Josh
m. Emma Bowen 1st m. Jack Bowen (D)
Sabrina
Jesse*
With Family in Mind
Special Edition #1450
on sale February 2002
Anything for Her Family
Silhouette Romance #1580
on sale March 2002
A Family To Be
Silhouette Romance #1586
on sale April 2002
A Family To Come Home To
Special Edition #1468
on sale May 2002
Symbols:
= Twins
d Deceased
D Divorced
* Kidnapped at age 5

Chapter One

Saddle Falls, Nevada

She was in trouble.

Josh Ryan instinctively knew it the moment he spotted Emma Bowen pacing the outer reception area of his second-floor law office. He may not have seen her in six years, but a lifelong friendship and a heart full of memories hadn't diminished his instincts when it came to Em.

Hell, she was practically family; the little sister he'd never had. As such, he'd always had special feelings for her and felt particularly protective of her.

And her very tender heart.

Something strong and instinctive rose within Josh, making him long to go to her, as he'd done when they'd been children, hauling her into his arms and holding her until the pain and fear he saw etched in her face—her eyes—eased.

But they weren't children any longer, Josh reminded himself. Six long years and a lot of water had run under the bridge.

He'd been trying to contact her for weeks—ever since her father's fatal heart attack a month ago—to no avail. His letters to her last address had come back, causing the first inklings of worry, and so, with no other choice, he'd hired an investigator.

Now, Em was here, and Josh was absolutely certain she was definitely in some kind of trouble.

What he didn't know was what he was going to do about it. Or more importantly, he thought with a sigh, what Em would *let* him do about it.

He had a feeling he was about to find out.

Struggling to hold back a bout of nausea and nervousness, pregnant Emma Bowen anxiously paced the carpeted reception area of the expansive law office that occupied the second floor of the Saddle Falls Hotel—the only hotel in town.

Early January sunlight filtered through the blinds of the spacious second-floor office, coating everything with a golden sheen. The Midas touch, she thought with a grin, and so absolutely fitting for Josh Ryan's law offices.

She'd never had any doubt that Josh would be a success at whatever he chose as a profession. Like his older brothers, Josh was quite simply the kind of man who'd succeed at *anything* he set his mind to. Personally or professionally.

"Em?" The gentle, masculine voice stopped her in her tracks. She didn't need to turn around to recognize the familiar voice from her childhood. Memories washed over her, along with an another unwanted wave of nausea. Resolutely, she swallowed hard and prayed the room would stop spinning. Fainting at Josh's feet was hardly the reunion she'd envisioned.

"Josh." Gathering her courage, Em took a slow, deep breath, prayed she could hold the nausea and dizziness at bay, then turned to him with a shaky smile, grateful her oversize sunglasses hid both her red-rimmed eyes and the dark circles under them.

"Oh Josh, it's so good to see you." Emotions flooded her and tears burned the backs of her eyes as she took his outstretched hands and gave them a grateful squeeze.

Josh looked every bit the successful, sophisticated attorney she'd envisioned in his three-piece gray pin-striped suit and Em tried not to feel intimidated by the gorgeous, elegant man standing in front of her.

This was Josh, she reminded herself, once her dearest, closest childhood friend. The kindest, gentlest person she'd ever known. There was no reason to feel intimidated.

Dear sweet Josh, Em thought again. Until this moment, she hadn't realized how much she'd missed him and his friendship.

From the moment he'd rescued her from a schoolyard bully when she was six years old, Josh had become her self-appointed protector, her confidant, her…*everything.* Including the family she desperately wanted—needed—but never had.

At least until his own parents' deaths and then a falling out had estranged Josh and Em until this very day.

"It's been a long time," Josh said, his smile gentle. "It's good to see you, too, Em. Although I'm sorry about the circumstances." Nodding quietly, Em removed her sunglasses to dab at her eyes. "I'm very sorry about your father, Em," Josh added. "I know you and he never got along, but...he did love you. In his own way," he added softly.

"Thanks, Josh," she said, dabbing at her eyes again, knowing Josh was just being kind. Not once in her life had she ever felt or believed her father had loved her, at least not since she was six and her mother died.

But then again, no one would know better than Josh about her strained relationship with her father. It was to Josh's house next door where she'd always run when her father's harsh criticisms became too much for her fragile, scarred heart.

While she was growing up, the Ryans had become her substitute family. And Josh, and his older brothers Jake and Jared had become like her big brothers.

"Em, are you okay?" Josh asked, putting his worry into words as he stepped closer to her. Her eyes were dulled by tears and grief, shadowed by circles that left her looking weary. And she was far too thin, he noted with alarm, glancing at the baggy, frayed jeans and oversize white blouse that practically dwarfed her. Her normally translucent complexion was even paler than he remembered, only increasing his worry.

Although she was all grown-up now, not the scared, insecure young girl he'd once known, she still reminded him of a very delicate, fragile porcelain doll. With her petite frame and small, feminine features, she'd always aroused every protective instinct he'd ever had.

At least that hadn't changed, Josh thought, looking at her more carefully. He had so many questions, and not nearly enough answers about her life and her circumstances, but at the moment the last thing he wanted to do was press her or pry. She didn't look as if she were up to it.

Something is wrong, he thought again. Something that had nothing to do with her father's death, he'd venture. He'd known Em far too long, and they'd been far too close for her to hide anything from him.

"Em?" His voice although quiet, held a question, and Em smiled, blowing a tangle of ebony bangs off her forehead.

"I'm fine, Josh," she lied, pressing a hand to her roiling stomach. "Really," she insisted, wishing her voice sounded more confident.

"Good," he said, not at all convinced. "Let's go into my office then, so we can talk." He took her elbow, surprised anew at how thin she was, and led her into his private sanctum, closing the door softly behind her. "Have a seat," he said, gesturing toward the long, leather couch set against the far wall. "Can I get you something?" he asked, glancing back at her over his shoulder as he rifled through the papers on his desk for her file. "A soft drink? A sandwich?"

"No, thanks, Josh. I'm fine." She wanted to roll her eyes at the mere thought of food. Ingesting something—*anything*—right now was enough to set her stomach roiling again.

Em sat back, glancing around the room. Impeccably decorated in shades of navy and alabaster, the walls were dotted with awards and diplomas as well as a host of family photographs, making the ache inside Em grow.

The only two things she'd ever wanted in her life were a family—and Josh Ryan.

She'd never gotten either.

"Em." Josh picked up a file off his desk and joined

her on the couch. ''I'm sorry it took so long for me to locate you—''

She waved away his apology with a trembling hand. ''No, Josh, I'm sorry it was so difficult to find me.'' She wasn't about to start explaining the horrendous events of her life during the past few months or how she'd been forced out of military housing when her husband of six years had abandoned her, going AWOL somewhere in Guam while on temporary assignment. She was far too embarrassed and ashamed to admit, especially to Josh, what a mess she'd made of her life.

Now, it was important for her to focus only on *why* she was here, back in Saddle Falls, and what she had to do to finally put her life in order. Curious, she cocked her head to look at him. ''How *did* you find me?''

He smiled. ''Your dad kept all of your letters with the return address. I knew the approximate area you were in, so I hired a private investigator.'' She nodded, surprised by the fact that her father had kept letters he'd never once answered, but not in the least bit surprised that Josh had the wherewithal to use them to locate her.

Josh flipped through the file folder, examining papers. ''Em, as your dad's attorney, he asked me to fulfill some of his final wishes.''

''Josh?'' Her voice was whisper soft, causing him to glance up at her.

''Yes, Em?''

''How—how did my father die?'' she asked quietly. She'd been notified after the fact, and after the final services had been completed so she had no idea of the circumstances.

"Oh, Em." Josh shook his head, remorse washing over him. He reached for her hand and held it tightly in his own, stunned by the coldness of her skin. "I'm sorry. I'd forgotten that my letter only gave you the very basic information." He hesitated, not wanting to make this any more painful for her than it already obviously was. He took a deep breath, then said, "Your father had a heart attack in his sleep. Doc Haggerty assured me that it was quite painless." His gaze searched her face, his own heart aching at the grief and sadness reflected in her eyes. "He didn't suffer, Em," Josh added softly as she nodded her acceptance. "He'd left specific instructions about his final arrangements, and as his attorney, Em, I was bound to honor them. I'm sorry I couldn't wait to locate you, but—"

"No, Josh, it's all right," she said, forcing a smile. "I understand. Under the circumstances you did the only thing you could." Her chin jutted. "You did what Daddy wanted and that's all that matters." And it was. They both knew how hardheaded and stubborn her father could be and she didn't think her father would have cared one way or the other whether she'd been there for the final services or not. The fact that it still hurt surprised her. She thought she'd come to terms with her father and their relationship. Apparently, she hadn't.

"But Em," Josh said, watching her carefully. "There are still some matters that will need your attention."

"I know." She grinned, trying to relax as he turned to her. "That's what your letter said. That's why I'm here." That, and the fact that she had absolutely nowhere else in the world to go.

''Em, your dad left you his house and the diner. Both are fully paid for—free and clear, as well as all his household furnishings and his car.'' He glanced at her again. ''Basically, he's left you everything.''

He laid the keys to her future in her empty hand and an overwhelming sense of relief swamped her, and Em nearly burst into tears.

Her daddy's house, and the diner.

Immediately, the image of the small ranch house that sat on a small plot of land that abutted the enormous Ryan ranch came to mind. The large country kitchen with the worn pine-board floors, where her mother used to bake the luscious homemade cakes and pies that had become the foundations of her father's diner. The large, sprawling living room with its rag rugs, stone fireplace and the large picture window overlooking the large, old-fashioned front porch. The three bedrooms down the narrow hallway—bedrooms that had seemed so cold and empty during her youth.

Her daddy's house.

In spite of the memories she'd rather forget, memories that had always made her father's house seem less than a home, no words had ever sounded sweeter to her. Now she had a place to live, and knowing her father had left her the diner, she also had a way to support herself.

It was as if she'd been given a gift from the heavens; from her father who'd never been there for her during her life, but somehow had provided for her in his death.

Although she was deeply grieved and remorseful about her father—she'd loved him even if she didn't understand him—his death, coming at a time when she was so desperate, and so very, very scared for herself and her baby had been a blessing in disguise.

Em's sigh was sad and weary, and she admonished herself not to start feeling sorry for herself, but to cherish this moment and this wonderful, generous gift her father had given her.

It took a moment for the true reality to sink in, and an enormous burden she'd been carrying alone for the past five months seemed to lift off her slender shoulders, freeing her from the fear and panic that had walked every step of the way with her every day of those five months.

Closing her eyes, she pressed a protective hand against her slightly bulging tummy, and said a silent, grateful prayer before taking some slow, deep breaths to contain both her tears and her emotions.

What she really wanted to do was jump with unbridled joy and relief.

But she knew she couldn't.

Josh would become alarmed and the last thing she wanted to do was alarm Josh, she thought in sudden amusement. Always the worrier, alarming Josh was tantamount to waving a red flag in front of an angry bull. It would only cause him to leap into action like some ultraresponsible television hero, to jump into the role of her rescuer and protector, something she couldn't—and wouldn't allow him to do.

Not anymore.

She was no longer a child, but an adult, and if her first encounter with Josh ended up with her weeping and wailing about life's misfortunes, or rather *her* misfortunes, Josh would think he'd have to take care of her, protect her, or worse, "fix" things for her.

And in spite of her situation, or maybe *because* of

it, Em knew that she was the only one who could fix things in her life.

This was her life, and she planned to take responsibility for it.

She knew it; and she had to be certain that when the time came, Josh knew it, too.

So, for now, she'd simply have to silently savor and rejoice in this generous bequest from her father and be grateful for the blessings bestowed on her.

Josh looked at her a moment, then gave in to the urges rushing through him and lifted a gentle hand to Emma's too pale cheek. Her skin seemed unusually cool and a bit clammy, worrying him further.

"Em?" He frowned, longing to just hold her in his arms, to offer the comfort he feared she sorely needed. "Are you sure you're all right?"

Em bit back a sigh. She simply wanted to lean into his comfort, his warmth, if only for a brief moment, if only to erase the terrible coldness and loneliness seeping through her, chilling her to the bone.

Get a grip, Em, she scolded herself. Daddy always told you never to spill your problems onto others. The least she could do under the circumstances was honor her father's wishes—at least once in her life. And not embarrass herself in the process.

"Em, look, if you're not up to this right now, we can do it later," Josh said. She looked so pale, so frail and fragile he feared she might keel over.

Nearly undone by his touch as well as his kindness, Em slowly shook her head, not trusting herself to speak, praying the wave of nausea and dizziness winding through her once again would pass. If only the room would stay still until she got this business over with, she'd be eternally grateful.

''I'm fine, Josh,'' she said, forcing a too bright and brittle smile, gritting her teeth and taking slow, deep breaths the way the doctor had instructed to keep the bile from rising in her throat, choking her. ''Really,'' she lied, placing a hand over her tummy again.

He nodded, not believing a word she said. There was obviously something drastically wrong here, something more than just her grief over her father. But he wasn't about to press the issue right now. There would be time for that—later. He hoped.

''Well, I'm sure you're tired from your trip. So why don't we do the rest of this later? There's no rush. Aggie's been handling the diner since your father's death, so she has those keys and things are going smoothly there so there's really nothing to worry about at the moment.'' He glanced at her again, trying to see beyond the carefully controlled facade she was trying to get him to accept. ''Are you going to be staying at your dad's house while you're here?'' he asked carefully. ''Or are you going back home right away.''

Home.

She'd come to believe there was no such thing, at least not for her.

''No,'' she said carefully, glancing down at her fingers carefully laced in her lap. ''I'm not going anywhere for a while.'' Smiling, she glanced up at him to find him watching her curiously. ''And yes, I'm going to be staying in Daddy's house while I'm here.''

''Then why don't I run you home so you can get yourself settled in?'' With a frown, Josh glanced down at the sheaf of papers in the folder. ''There's still a few more things we need to go over, but they can wait,'' he said as he closed the file.

For a moment, Em hesitated, torn between wanting to get this over with, and wanting to find someplace cool and quiet to rest. She'd been traveling nearly eighteen hours on a bus in order to get here, and right now, her head was throbbing like a bongo drum being abused by a recalcitrant toddler, and the dizziness rocking every inch of her body was just magnifying everything else.

To say she'd had better days was surely an understatement. At the moment, she just wanted to find someplace to lay her head down and put up her aching feet. Then, she'd think about getting something in her stomach. Maybe this time it just might surprise her and stay there.

''Later is fine, Josh. But there's no need for you to take me home. I don't want to interrupt your day.'' Nor did she want to start becoming dependent on Josh again. No, *independence* was the word of the day, especially when it came to Josh.

''Really Em, it's no trouble. I'd be happy to do it.'' He wasn't certain he liked the idea of just letting her walk out of his office right now, and certainly not alone.

''I know, Josh.'' Grateful, she laid a hand on his arm. ''And I appreciate it, I truly do, but I think I might enjoy the walk,'' she said with a sassy smile. ''To get acquainted with the town again.'' Absently, she walked to the large glass window that fronted the main street of Saddle Falls, and immediately a well of memories sprang to life. She could see the Saddle Falls movie theater marquee, as well as the sign for a new pizzeria just across the street. If she craned her neck, she could almost see her father's diner just a short way down. With a sigh, she turned back to Josh. "How's your family, Josh? Your grandfather, Tommy? Your brothers?" *You,* she wanted to ask, but didn't.

His grin was quick and charming. "Tommy's fine, as always. He's pushing eighty but you'd never know it. Jake got married about a few months ago, and Jared followed suit shortly thereafter." He lifted a finger to scratch a brow. "Rebecca, Jake's wife, is expecting, and also Natalie, Jared's wife." He laughed. "They already have a set of twins with another set on the way."

"Twins?" She grinned. "Tommy must be thrilled," she said, knowing how his grandfather Tommy felt about family.

Josh nodded, thinking about the one person they didn't talk about—his brother Jesse who had been kidnapped from their own home almost twenty years ago, never to be heard from again.

"And what about you, Josh?" she asked softly, ignoring the increased tempo of her heart. "Have you taken the plunge yet?"

He shook his head. "Not me," he answered with a shake of his head and another quick grin. "Someone's got to hold up the Ryan hell-raising tradition. I figure it's my responsibility now. I'm the last unmarried Ryan and I wouldn't want to deprive the town gossips of their daily news fix."

That brought another smile to Em's face as memories from her childhood surfaced. One thing about small town living. Everyone knew everyone else's business. It would be a relief to be living among people she knew once again, rather than living in a community of strangers who didn't know or care about one another.

Josh glanced around his spacious office, pride evident in his face. ''Anyway, I'm too busy to get married, Em. I've got my practice to handle and I'm still managing the hotel as well as several other properties the family owns. My time really is taken,'' he said. ''I converted the top floor of the hotel into an apartment for myself so I don't have to keep running back and forth to the ranch, but I still go home to the ranch at least twice a week for dinner and to see the family.''

The family. *His* family. For so long the Ryans had made Emma feel like family as well. Until this moment, she hadn't realized how much she'd missed or loved this little town and everything and everyone in it. But then again, she knew she'd never have felt this way if she hadn't left.

Sometimes you had to lose something in order to truly appreciate it, she thought with a sigh.

''So, to be honest, Em I wouldn't mind running you home. It'll give me a chance to stop and see Tommy.''

''Thanks, Josh,'' she said with a firm shake of her head. ''But I think a walk through town might be just what I need right now. Besides,'' she added with a laugh when she saw he was still frowning. ''I can walk to my father's house from here in less time than it will take you to start your car and drive it out of the parking lot. I'll be fine, Josh, truly.'' It was her turn to lay a hand to his cheek. ''Please don't worry about me, Josh.''

''All right, Em,'' he said with a nod, not in the least bit convinced. How on earth did she expect him *not* to worry when she looked like a good, brisk wind would knock her over?

Again, he bit his tongue, refusing to pry. She had enough on her plate right now, coming to terms with her father's death, not to mention whatever else was troubling her. Whatever it was, it was *big,* he realized, something she couldn't hide from him. But then again, Em never had been able to hide anything from him. They'd always been far too close. Like two matched peas in a pod.

But he didn't want to push her now, didn't want to start prying into something until he was certain she was up to answering his questions. "I'll stop by later to see you. We can go over the rest of the details then."

"Fine." On impulse, Emma leaned up on tiptoe and kissed his cheek. "Thanks, Josh. For everything." Her gaze searched his and she felt her aching heart soften and tumble over. *Dear Josh.* Even after all these years he was still the solid rock of stability she'd come to love as a child. At least some things never changed, she thought with an inner smile. "You have no idea how good it is to see you."

"And you, Em," he said softly. Unable to conceal his concern, Josh dragged a hand through his hair. "In the meantime, if you need anything, anything at all, you just give a holler, you hear?"

"I hear," she said with a smile.

Reluctant to just let her leave, Josh struggled to find something else to say, to keep her there if only for a few more moments to soothe his own worried mind. "Em—" Unable to resist, he dropped his hands to her slender shoulders, felt them shaking, then pulled her close for a quick hug of comfort, not certain if it was more for his sake or hers.

The sweet scent of her perfume, something that smelled like fresh-picked roses coupled with a hint of vanilla teased his nostrils, making him vividly aware of her and the fact that she was no longer a little girl. And if her scent wasn't enough to remind him, surely the lush, feminine body pressed tightly against him certainly would have.

She *had* grown up on him, he realized with a start, although she really hadn't changed all that much. She still had that short cap of unruly black hair that framed a delicate, porcelain face. And what a face, he thought with a smile. Em had matured into quite a beauty. Her eyes were huge and the color of deep sapphires, ringed by long fringes of dark lashes.

With her small, sassy mouth and that cute upturned nose dotted with a mass of freckles, she still reminded him of a precious doll. But that oversize shirt she had on coupled with those baggy jeans made her looked even more delicate; her clothes swamped her.

Closing his eyes, Josh tried to put all worry out of his mind, and simply held Emma, grateful to have her home once again. He had indeed missed her, missed her friendship and her closeness. Emma had been the one and only woman, other than his mother, he'd ever trusted.

Except for one painful exception, he thought, his face clouding with grief. *Melanie.* No, he wasn't going to ruin this moment by thinking of her and what she'd done. Not now. Now, he was merely going to enjoy the present.

With Josh's strong, gentle hands caressing her back, for just a moment, Em allowed herself to lean into him, to feel the warmth of his comfort and concern. It had been so long since she'd had the care of comfort of another person she felt as if she were drowning in long-suppressed emotions.

She wanted to abandon herself to the feelings, to merely cling to Josh and his strength and comfort, to share the pain and burdens she'd carried the past few months.

But she couldn't and she knew it.

Stunned by the impact of having that hard, masculine body pressed so intimately against her, and fearing Josh might discover her secret, Em forced herself to draw back, to look up at him. Way up. He'd always towered over her; now that he was full grown, he did so more than ever. The man had to top at least six-four, maybe even six-five.

Goodness, Emma thought, with a grin, he'd grown up to be undeniably gorgeous. She shook her head, amused at herself and the fact that even after all these years, she still found her childhood friend so mouth-wateringly appealing.

He may have been all grown-up now, and all spiff and polish as only fitting Saddle Falls's most prominent attorney, but he still had those wild Irish blue eyes that always hinted at a bit of rebellion and mischief and a shock of coal-black hair that was styled in such a way to give him a reckless, slightly dangerous look—respected attorney or not.

While all the Ryan boys were incredibly gorgeous, setting female hearts aflutter all over town, there'd always been something just a bit special about Josh.

Perhaps it was his confidence or maybe it was the hint of mischief always lurking behind his incredible eyes, or maybe it was the unending kindness and generosity of his heart and his spirit, especially for those he loved.

Whatever it was that Josh had, Em was sure glad she was immune to a man's charm now—immune and cured, otherwise she could be in serious female-heart trouble here.

But she wasn't, she assured herself confidently. Josh was, and always had been just a friend. Hadn't he made that abundantly clear when she was twelve and he was fourteen and in a fit of female stupidity she'd confessed her undying love for him?

She'd been hurt by his rejection, hurt that he'd dismissed her feelings as those of just a kid, so hurt that she'd decided then and there never to let him know how she truly felt about him ever again.

It was a promise she'd kept. And intended to keep.

She might have been a slow learner as her father had always told her, but she wasn't *stupid.*

Besides, she'd fallen in love with a man once, then foolishly married him, believing she could have a romantic fairy-tale life. But she knew now what it had cost her; she was not about to make that mistake ever again. She wasn't about to let herself be blinded by love ever again. Especially with a man who'd already told her he'd never love *her* that way.

But boy, it sure didn't hurt to look, she decided in amusement, suddenly tickled by the fact that Josh was—as always—worrying. She could see it in his eyes, in the set of his strong chin.

Em sighed, realizing that some things never changed. And Josh's propensity for worrying about her was one. But she couldn't help but feel totally charmed and enchanted by it, knowing that Josh was still…Josh, and that brought about a certain sense of comfort and security in what, up to now, had been a very insecure world to her.

Her father's generosity had solved every immediate problem she had, so much so, that she could actually smile and mean it.

But having Josh's arms around her was playing havoc with her pulse and her tumultuous emotions—not a good thing in her condition.

"Em, I'm glad you're home."

She beamed at him allowing the first honest emotion to cut through the haze of fear and panic that had walked with her for months. "So am I, Josh. So am I." With a regretful little sigh, Em stepped back out of his embrace, not trusting the feelings and emotions Josh's touch had evoked. It was just hormones, she told herself, trying not to get too excited by the feelings suffusing her. The doctor said it would happen, had in fact told her to expect it. So the feelings Josh's touch evoked was certainly nothing to get alarmed about. Nothing at all.

"Thanks, Josh, for everything. I'll see you later." Anxious to leave because of how she was feeling, Em headed toward the door, holding back her sigh of unbridled relief until Josh's office door closed quietly behind her.

Chapter Two

Two hours later, juggling a bag of groceries, a small suitcase and her purse, Emma nervously inserted her key into the front door, and for the first time in six long years stepped into her father's house.

Although it was January, the days in Nevada were still warm, but the house had been closed up and the air-conditioning turned off, so that now the house was eerily dark and stifling oppressive, making it difficult to breathe. With the front door still open, allowing a hint of light from the fading sun, inside Emma leaned on the doorjamb, letting everything in her arms slide to the floor as another bout of nausea and dizziness hit her. The grocery bag tipped, dumping its contents onto the floor where cans rolled and boxes bounced across the room. Watching them, Em merely shook her head, unable to drag up enough energy to go chasing after them.

She was already in her second trimester of pregnancy and the doctors had assured her this lightheadedness, along with the morning sickness and unbearable fatigue would have passed by now.

Clearly, they'd been wrong, she thought with a frown, unconsciously pressing a protective hand against her slightly bulging tummy.

Totally drained, she leaned her back against the door, then slid down until her behind reached the floor, not trusting her shaky legs to support her any longer.

Staying utterly still, she kept her eyes closed until that cold, clammy feeling passed and the room finally stopped spinning.

After swallowing convulsively several times, Emma opened her eyes, rubbed them, then glanced around the once familiar house, outlined now in mere shadows by the darkness. A wealth of emotions and memories seemed to spring to life, as if the mere act of stepping back inside her father's house had finally released them.

It was hard to believe she was actually home.

Home.

Tears filled her eyes, and she furiously blinked them away. It had been a long, long time since she'd thought of this house as a *home.* Not since her mother died when she was barely six years old.

After that, everything had changed, especially her father, who had no patience for a lonely little girl's tears or fears. If Emma closed her eyes, she could still hear his deep, gruff voice echoing through the house.

''You're eight years old, girl, time for you to grow up. The dark ain't nothing to be afraid of. So stop that sniveling and go to sleep before I give you something to snivel about.''

Emma pushed her hair off her face, then blew out

a breath. She supposed her father was suffering from his own form of grief, but at the time she wasn't old enough to understand that he might be hurting as well. All she knew was her own fear and pain—which was so huge it seemed to have cut a life-size hole in her heart—had never really healed.

With a sigh, she rubbed her hands over her weary eyes again, letting them slide closed for a moment, trying not to feel sorry for herself. But every time she closed her eyes she could hear her father's voice.

Don't you go crying to the Ryans anymore, you hear me Em? I won't have any daughter of mine telling tales about me to our neighbors. You got a good life, girl, a roof over your head and food on the table. So stop your complaining, you hear me?

Lord, she thought with a shake of her head, how her father had resented the Ryans for giving her the comfort—the sense of belonging and family—he wasn't able to. If she hadn't known better, she would have sworn he was almost relieved when Josh's parents had been killed in a plane crash.

With Mrs. Ryan gone, she'd gone back to living with the loneliness, tension and fear that had dogged her from the time she was six, until she'd finally escaped her father's house at twenty.

Escaped.

Emma smiled sadly. It was hard to believe she still thought of leaving her father's house as escaping, but she did. It had been six long years since she'd ran out this very door, tears spilling down her cheeks, her father's harsh, angry words ringing in her ears.

That boy's no good, girl. I'm telling you. You marry him and you'll bring on nothing but heartache. He'll give you a belly-full then run at the first sign of trouble. And then what? Don't think you can come crying home to me. If you leave now, don't you ever come back, you hear me, girl? You won't be welcome in my home.

"I heard you, Daddy," Emma whispered, choking back a sob as her voice echoed along the walls of the empty house. "I heard you." At the time, she had no idea those would be the last words her father would ever say to her. Or how true they would turn out to be. "You were right this time, Daddy," she said with a sniffle. "That boy *was* no good. No good at all." Unfortunately, it had taken her almost six years of marriage and one pregnancy to discover it.

Emma tried to shake off the terror that had invaded her battered heart and nearly broken her spirit during the months following Jack's abandonment when she was alone and pregnant with nowhere to live and no one to turn to, and worse, no way to support or take care of her precious child.

And she wondered again how she could have been so naive? So foolish?

Clearly, foolishly loving a man had led her to lose any sense of judgment. Loving a man, and allowing herself to trust and *depend* on him was what had gotten her into this mess of a situation in the first place.

She was not about to make that mistake ever again. She wasn't about to let herself be blinded by love ever again.

Glancing around the room and feeling a profound sense of relief for the first time in months, Em grinned, rubbing her belly. "You and me, Baby Girl, we're gonna be just fine now. Just fine, love."

Suddenly too weary to even keep her eyes open any longer, Em leaned her head back against the door, closed her eyes and allowed herself just a few moments of self-indulgence to savor the sense of peace and security she finally felt.

''Oh, my God, Em!'' Standing at the foot of the porch stairs, Josh could see her crumpled on the floor through the open doorway. He'd left the office early, feeling as if he needed to check up on her. Now, he was glad he had.

Without thought, he took the stairs two at a time, his heart pumping in overtime. ''Em, good Lord, what happened? Are you all right?'' His gaze took in the scattered groceries, her overturned purse, and her keeled over suitcase, and his fear grew. ''I knew I should never have let you walk out of my office alone.'' Without giving her a chance to explain, he bent, scooped her up in his arms, and cradled her close.

''Josh.'' Trying to catch her breath, she laid a hand to his chest, both touched and amused by his concern and alarm. ''Josh, please, put me down. I'm fine, really.'' She managed a weak smile as she glanced up at him.

''Yeah, and I'm Big Bird,'' he growled, storming across the darkened living room, kicking cans and boxes out of his way.

Emma couldn't help it, she started to laugh. ''You're the wrong color, Josh,'' she teased, burying her face in his shoulder. ''But about the right height.''

''This is not funny, Emma,'' he scolded, using her full given name to show his annoyance as he gently laid her down on the couch, before snatching a toss pillow from an adjacent chair to tenderly tuck under her head. ''Not funny at all,'' he declared, glaring down at her from troubled eyes. "You scared the life out of me." For a moment, he merely stood over her, not certain what to do. "Are you sick, Em? Should I call Doc Haggerty?" he finally asked with a frown.

"No, Josh. I don't need Doc Haggerty and I'm not sick." It wasn't a lie, she told herself. She was *pregnant,* not sick. But she wanted to avoid the moment when she had to tell Josh, knowing his reaction would give the word *panic* whole new meaning.

Scowling, Josh planted his hands on his hips, glaring down at her, unwilling to let her stonewall him any longer. "Then do you mind telling me why the heck you were sprawled on the floor, white as a ghost?"

She shrugged, trying to make light of it. "I guess I'm just...hungry," she hedged with a rueful smile. "That's all. And I got a bit dizzy so I just sat down." She shrugged, aware that he looked as if he wasn't buying her story, not one bit.

"Hungry?" His scowl deepened. "When was the last time you had something to eat?"

She was quiet for a moment, chewing her bottom lip while she thought about the question, making him sigh heavily again. "Yesterday, I think."

Yesterday? He wanted to growl under his breath. Didn't she even have enough sense to eat properly? That would certainly explain why she was so thin, he thought.

"You *think,*" he repeated in exasperation, giving his head a shake. "No wonder you can barely stand upright. You just stay right where you are, Em, do you hear me?"

"Yes, Josh," she said in amusement, knowing

there was no point in arguing with him when he had that look on his face.

He moved around the house, turning on lights, flipping on the air-conditioning, gathering up her scattered groceries.

He'd changed from the custom-tailored suit he'd worn this afternoon, and now had on a pair of faded jeans worn white in spots—jeans that hugged those magnificently masculine legs and thighs—and a white T-shirt that stretched far and wide to cover his broad chest and wide shoulders. The white contrasted sharply with the deeply bronzed tan he wore year-round, which she knew came from helping his brother Jared out on their ranch.

"Josh, if you wouldn't mind bringing that chocolate ice cream over here, I'd appreciate it."

He glanced down at the carton in his arms, then at her. Her eyes were twinkling and some of her color had returned. She didn't look nearly so shaky, making him feel a bit better.

He walked into the kitchen, got a spoon from a drawer, then came back to her, popping off the top of the ice cream carton before handing it, along with the spoon to her.

"This is not exactly my idea of nourishment," he commented, watching as she dipped the spoon into the creamy confection. "But if you share, I might not complain," he added with a grin, sitting down next to her. At least the ice cream had sugar and would hopefully give her a boost of energy, he thought, watching as she dipped her spoon into the ice cream and fed him a bite, aware that his gaze never left hers.

"Em, look, I know I told you there were some additional details to handle regarding your father's last wishes, and I thought they could wait, but—'' He broke off, dragging a hand through his hair, not wanting to press her, but wanting to give her some assurance that things on his end were properly handled.

''But what, Josh?'' she asked, taking another bite of the ice cream and nearly sighing in pleasure as the icy coolness exploded on her tongue.

''But, maybe we'd better get this taken care of now.'' He hesitated. ''I don't know what your plans are, Em, or how long you plan to stay in Saddle Falls, but I don't want you worrying about things on this end. I've got everything taken care of. Your dad asked me to handle the sale of this house and the diner for you. Now, I've already assembled a list of prospective buyers and I'm just qualifying them now so it shouldn't be long—''

''*Sell* the diner and the house?'' Em almost choked on her ice cream. She turned to Josh stunned by his words, as well as his closeness. He was so near she could see her own pale reflection in his eyes. Her pulse kicked up, surprising her. Hormones, she assured herself. Just hormones. ''Why on earth would I want to sell the diner and this house?'' The house and diner were all she had to secure her baby's future. She had no intention of selling anything.

Josh shrugged, reaching for her spoon to help himself to some more ice cream. ''Well, I guess your dad just assumed that you and your husband wouldn't want the hassle of a house and a business, especially since you move around so much from base to base.'' Josh shrugged. ''I imagine your dad just wanted to make things easier for you.''

Never in her life had her father ever cared or tried

to make anything easier for her, but she didn't see the need to point that out right now. "Josh?"

"Hmm?" He stopped spooning ice cream from the carton to look at her. Something in her face set off an internal alarm bell inside him. "What Em?"

"Josh," she began carefully, glancing around and feeling an uncommon sense of security and comfort at being around so many familiar things. It was a feeling that had eluded her for a very long time and now she merely wanted to savor it. "First of all, I'm not married, at least not anymore," she added, rushing on as shock registered on his face. "And as much as I appreciate all your hard work, I have no intention of selling either this house or the diner. Not now," she added firmly. "Not ever."

"Okay," he said slowly. "Then maybe you'd better tell me just what your plans are?"

She hesitated, then grinned, placing a loving hand over her belly. "Well, me and Baby Cakes plan on staying right here in Saddle Falls, living in Daddy's house and running the diner." She grinned up into his stunned face. "That's the plan." She reached for her spoon, but Josh hung on tight.

"Uh...Em," he began cautiously. "Who is Baby Cakes?"

"The baby, Josh."

"Baby?" he repeated as if he'd never heard the word before, making her laugh.

"*My* baby, Josh." Maternal pride glowed in her face as he gaped at her in utter shock. "I'm having a baby, Josh." Reaching for his hand, she placed it on her slightly swollen belly. He snatched it back as if she'd stuck it into a burning flame.

"You're having a *baby?*" he repeated in alarm, glancing at her belly. *"Now?"*

"Well, thankfully not at the moment," she said with another laugh. "I'm a bit worn-out today, but the doctor says Baby Cakes should be arriving in about four months—give or take a week."

"Four months?" Josh repeated dully, glancing at her belly again, then quickly lifting his stunned gaze to hers as he did the calculations. "Em, that's only sixteen weeks away."

He rubbed his forehead where a tension headache had started. "Em, are you telling me you're alone *and* pregnant?" he asked as every implication, problem and complication of being alone and pregnant marched through his legal mind, one by one, only intensifying his alarm.

"Yep, Josh, I imagine that's what I'm telling you," she said with a grin, amused by his apparent panic.

"Em, this isn't funny," he said in a tone of voice that made her roll her eyes. She knew better than anyone that her situation wasn't funny. She'd lived through it and knew she hadn't exactly had a barrel of laughs the past few months, and she really didn't need Josh pointing out the fact to her.

"No, it isn't, Josh," she said carefully, bracing a hand on the couch seat as another bout of dizziness hit. She took a slow, deep breath. "What's funny is your reaction. I'm not the first woman to have a baby on her own, and I'd bet I won't be the last, either."

"Yeah, but Em..." Exasperated, his voice trailed off and he shook his head, scrubbing his hands over his face. For an instant, another single pregnant woman flashed through his mind; a woman who had been too wrapped up in her career to have time or concern for her unborn child. So she'd merely... disposed of the child so she wouldn't have to be bothered.

His child, he thought bitterly, the pain and loss still so fresh after all this time it stunned him. He'd wanted his child, wanted the baby's mother as well, but Melanie hadn't wanted either of them, only her precious law career. She'd rebuffed his help, and his love, choosing instead to destroy the child he'd believed had been created in love.

He'd allowed himself to love her—and she'd betrayed him in a most hurtful way, hitting at the heart of him, destroying both his child and his love for her, as well as his ability to ever trust a woman again.

Banishing his own painful memories, Josh blew out a breath. "Em, where on earth is the baby's father?" he demanded, unable to stop the anger from seeping into his voice. "And why isn't he here taking care of you and the baby?"

"Well," Em said with a little sigh, trying to make light of the situation. "Last I heard he was somewhere in Guam." She shrugged, toying with the blanket Josh had earlier tossed over her. "But knowing Jack, he could be just about anywhere."

"Guam?" Josh repeated as if he hadn't quite heard her correctly. Realizing he had, his rare but real Irish temper blew. "Em, what the hell is the man doing in Guam?"

She shrugged again, trying not to grind her teeth together at his tone. "Well, Josh, that's a question I guess you, me and the United States Army might all like answered." She glanced down at her jeans, smoothing out a wrinkle, trying not to show how much simply saying the words aloud—admitting

Jack's abandonment—hurt. "About five months ago, he went to Guam on temporary duty assignment." She shrugged. "That's the last I heard from him. Apparently he went AWOL. No one's heard from him since."

A muscle in his jaw jerked, and his gaze narrowed. "Doesn't he know about the baby?"

"Yes, Josh, he knows," she said, forcing herself to meet his gaze, aware of the sadness and shame rolling over her. Admitting that her husband didn't want *her* was one thing, admitting he didn't want their *baby* was quite another. It hurt worse than she'd imagined.

"Are you telling me he took off because he didn't want his own child?" Josh asked in a deliberately quiet voice. A voice that, as kids, everyone in town knew was trouble. Em wanted to sigh again.

"Yes, Josh, that's exactly what I'm telling you." She laced her hands together in her lap so he wouldn't see them trembling.

"He just abandoned you and the baby?" The idea was so simply inconceivable to Josh he couldn't seem to comprehend how anyone could do something so incredibly despicable.

The look that swept over Em's features was more than enough of an answer for him and Josh felt something deep and foreign tug at his heart.

How on earth could a man just go off and leave his wife and unborn child to fend for themselves? he wondered. What kind of man abandoned his pregnant wife and child?

Scrubbing a hand over his face again, trying to garner some control, Josh realized this was not something he could ever even fathom, let alone understand.

The notion was so against everything he believed that he simply couldn't comprehend it.

As a Ryan, he'd grown up knowing—believing that family was everything. Perhaps that's why Melanie's actions had been so devastating to him, so much so that to this day he still hadn't gotten over it, still grieved for the child he'd never even been given a chance to know or love.

He'd never been able to forgive Melanie for destroying their child, or himself for not protecting it.

But to know that Em's husband had so callously and carelessly walked away from her knowing she was expecting, well, the man deserved to be shot. At the very least.

"Em, why?" He had to know, had to try to understand why and how a man could do something like this to his own wife, the one person in the world he should have loved and protected more than anyone else. "Why on earth would your husband just abandon you and the baby?"

"I'm not sure, Josh. Jack wasn't exactly what you'd call great father material," she admitted honestly. "Nor great husband material if you want to know the truth." With a sigh, she dragged a hand through her hair. "When I ran off to marry him, I thought for sure I was finally going to have the home and family I wanted." Her smile was sad and rueful, making Josh reach for her hand. "I realized too late that what I was really doing was running away from Daddy. Little did I know I was running from the frying pan into the fire." She forced a bright smile. "But I took a vow, Josh." She shrugged. "And I intended to honor it. I thought I could make it work."

"But it didn't?" he asked quietly.

"Not by a long shot," she admitted. "Of course, it would have if I wouldn't have minded the other women and the partying—"

Josh's gaze narrowed and unconsciously his fists clenched. "He cheated on you?" he said in a tone of voice that was so shocked she wanted to give him a pat in comfort. Knowing how the Ryan boys were all raised to believe that family and marriage was sacred, cheating on your spouse was not something that would ever enter their minds. Or be condoned or tolerated. Too bad Jack didn't have the same ideals.

"Right from the beginning," she admitted, wondering why it no longer hurt. "It didn't take me long to realize I'd made a mistake. But you know how I feel about marriage and family." Blowing out a pent-up breath, Em shoved a wad of bangs out of her eyes, unwilling to admit that at the time, she'd wanted the fairy tale, the home and loving family she'd never had enough to overlook Jack's blatant behavior. And at the time, she'd blamed herself for her husband's infidelities. She thought if she'd been a better wife, a better lover...Em's thoughts broke off and she clenched her hands together in her lap. No, she wasn't going to do that ever again. Never again would she accept responsibility for someone else's actions.

It had taken her several years to realize her husband's shortcomings had nothing to do with her as a person or a woman. He'd merely used her as an excuse for his inexcusable behavior. Perhaps if she'd been older or wiser, perhaps if she hadn't clung to the belief that the fairy tale was out there and she could have it if she just tried harder, she would have realized the reality of the situation sooner and saved herself years of grief.

"I understand, Em," Josh said quietly, his heart aching for her. Knowing how important, how sacred marriage and family were to her, her husband's disregard for their marriage vows must have been a crippling blow to her.

"Well, when I got pregnant, I was thrilled," she said, her eyes glowing happily. "You know how I feel about children." Some of the light dimmed in her eyes. "I thought for certain it was just the thing to make Jack grow up and see exactly how wonderful having a family could be. I thought for sure he would finally settle down."

"Apparently he had other ideas," Josh commented.

She nodded. "While I was thrilled about the baby, Jack on the other hand was afraid a baby might cramp his...lifestyle," Em added, unwilling to make excuses for her ex-husband any longer.

"Cramp his life—" Josh broke off, muttering a few oaths under his breath. "So basically, he didn't want the baby, is that it?"

"In a nutshell," Em admitted with a weary sigh.

"Em, when did this happen? I mean, how long ago did he abandon you?"

"Right after I told him I was pregnant." She shrugged, glancing across the room. "About five months ago to be exact."

His gaze searched hers. "What did you do?" he asked quietly, knowing she hadn't gone to her father for help.

She shrugged. "The best I could, Josh. Once it was confirmed that Jack had indeed gone AWOL, I was ordered out of military housing."

"They kicked you out of your home?" Josh asked.

"Well, Josh, the military sort of considered it their

home, and yes, to answer your question. I was asked—actually ordered—to move out of military housing. And with Jack AWOL obviously there was no paycheck coming in...." Her voice trailed off. She was unable to even think about that horrible time and the panic and fear she'd endured. "I'd talked to Jack's commanding officer, but finding one AWOL soldier is hardly at the top of the list of the army's priorities." She shrugged. "They promised to keep me informed if he was located, but that was about all they could do. So, I had no choice. I filed for divorce on the grounds of abandonment, moved out of military housing and tried to find some kind of work. I—I was having morning sickness really bad, even more so in the beginning than now, so I couldn't hold a job, and—" She stopped when Josh held up his hand.

He didn't think he could bear to hear the anguish she'd gone through, knowing she was alone and terrified, with no one to turn to, no one to count on during what should have been the happiest time of her life. He didn't think he could bear to see the fear and terror in her eyes, a fear and terror she was trying to hide behind some kind of false bravado that was only annoying him to no end.

If her ex-husband was smart, he'd stay in Guam, Josh thought, his fists clenching unconsciously. It would save him the trouble of...teaching him a lesson in responsibility.

"Em, I'm sorry, I truly am." He wanted to grab her up and hold her, to soothe the pain and hurt and the remaining fear in her eyes. "Why didn't you come home?"

"Home?" She laughed, but the sound was soft and bitter. "Josh, I never had a home, remember? When

I told my father I was dropping out of college to marry Jack, he warned me that Jack was no good, that if I went through with the marriage, I couldn't come crying to him when it went bad.'' She blinked back tears. ''He told me if I left that day I could never come home again.'' Sniffling, she swiped her nose, snuggling deeper into the couch. ''He meant it, Josh.''

''Em,'' Josh said, knowing he couldn't argue with her because what she'd said was true. Her father had been a bitter, cold man, incapable of showing love, but Josh had always believed in his own way that Em's father *had* loved her. ''You could have called me.'' Tenderly, he stroked a hand down her hair. ''You could always come to me, Em, you know that. No matter what.''

Hearing the words only made the tears flow faster because she knew Josh meant them. *Dear, sweet Josh.* No matter what, he'd always been there for her regardless of the circumstances, and she loved him for it.

''I suppose on some level I knew that, Josh. Truly,'' she added when he frowned. ''But you have to understand something. I'm not a little girl anymore. I'm an adult, Josh, a fully functioning capable adult about to become a mother. And I figured it was time I finally stood up on my own two feet.''

Never again would she depend on a man for her happiness or security, nor for her child's. She would take care of her child herself. And do a fine job of it as well, she thought firmly.

''Yeah, but Em, be reasonable here—''

''Reasonable?'' One brow rose at his tone. She knew where this was going and wanted to head him off at the pass. ''Josh, listen to me. I appreciate your concern. Truly I do,'' she added, touching his arm. ''But I don't need Jack or any other man, and neither does the baby. I am quite capable of taking care of myself and my baby. I'm going to have my baby, run the diner, *and* live in Daddy's house.'' Slowly she began to rub her stomach, feeling a strong, maternal connection to her precious child. ''I'll make a home for myself and my child on my own without anyone's help,'' she added softly.

Josh pressed his palms together and prayed for patience. No wonder Em looked so pale, so fragile, so unbearably vulnerable. After what she'd been through… Unable to even bear thinking about it, Josh blew out a frustrated breath.

Now that her father was gone, and her husband as well, she was totally alone, with no support system, no backup. No one to help or support her, either financially or emotionally.

The thought caused the protective instincts that had stirred earlier in the day to intensify and Josh had the urge to throttle the man who had put Em in this position.

She obviously had no idea what she was in for, obviously hadn't had time to think this through. She was probably just in shock. With her husband's abandonment and then her father's death, no wonder she didn't realize the absolute seriousness of her situation.

''Em, listen to me, I really don't think it's wise for you to even think about running the diner in your condition. I have a couple of good prospects who are interested in buying the—''

''My *condition?*'' she repeated slowly, a flush of anger warming her face. ''Josh, I'm *pregnant.* Not incompetent or incapacitated. I'm a perfectly healthy, normal woman, and there's absolutely no reason why I can't run the diner *and* have a baby. One doesn't necessary preclude the other. Millions of single women continue working while they're pregnant. It's not that big of a deal nowadays, Josh. In case you haven't heard.''

''But—''

''But nothing, Josh,'' she said, unable to contain her annoyance any longer. She was going on sheer nerves and adrenaline right now, and she wasn't up to having Josh or anyone else scrutinize or judge her actions. She was doing the best she could under difficult circumstances, and for now, it would simply have to be enough. ''I fully intend to run the diner, and have my baby—at the same time, Josh, whether you or anyone else like it, or approve of it or not!''

Chapter Three

Like most small towns, Saddle Falls had a rhythm and pattern to life, a predictability that provided a sense of security and stability. Everyone in town knew that at precisely 9:00 a.m. every weekday Matthew Able would check his pocket watch before unlocking the double doors to the one and only Saddle Falls bank. Virginia Wilson, the longtime town librarian, would follow suit, waiting until she saw Mr. Abel's Open sign before unlocking the doors to the town library. Perry's Grocery would open for business shortly thereafter, while Mr. Benedetto's fruit stand would be nearly empty by nine, having opened shortly after six so that busy wives and mothers would be able to purchase fruits and vegetables needed for that day's breakfast and lunches.

The Saddle Falls Diner, which sat opposite the movie theatre, and nearly kitty-corner from the hotel, was open five days a week from 5:00 a.m. until 3 p.m., serving home-cooked breakfasts and lunches.

Each day there was a soup of the day and a luncheon special, as well as a rash of homemade pies and cakes using Em's late mother's recipes.

Within a week of returning to town, news had spread that Emma Bowen was back home, pregnant but apparently minus one husband, running the diner and causing an increase in business, as it seemed everyone in town wanted to stop by to say hello.

If the scandal she'd caused when she ran off to get married six years before was still on people's minds, they politely didn't mention it. Instead, they preferred to express their sorrow at the loss of her father who'd been such an important part of the town.

After her first full week home, Em almost felt as if she hadn't left. She'd quickly fallen into the routine of the diner, thrilled at having something productive to do with herself and her time, knowing full well that each day that passed was more secure for herself and her child.

Every day Josh stopped in for breakfast and lunch, and never failed to use the opportunity to try to talk some sense into her, to at least listen to his offers for the diner and the house, but she refused. Her mind was made up.

This morning as she bustled around the busy diner, helping her father's longtime waitress-manager Agnes handle the early-morning breakfast rush, Josh trailed along behind her like a shadow.

"Be reasonable, Em," Josh said, dogging her steps. "You can't honestly think you can continue to handle working here, Em. I mean look at this place." Em grinned in pleasure as he glanced around. "It's mobbed," Josh complained.

"Yes, I know," she said, still grinning. "And

hopefully it will stay that way,'' she said, sidestepping around Josh to grab a fresh white apron from a stack behind the counter.

''But, Em you're *pregnant,*'' he reminded her again, putting a great deal more emphasis on the word than necessary, and garnering the attention of several customers in nearby booths.

''Thank you for pointing out the obvious, Josh,'' Em said, as she tied her apron on and then rounded the counter and grabbed a full pot of decaf coffee to start refilling cups. ''But I'm well aware of my condition.'' She hesitated, realizing he was still trailing after her. ''Josh, will you do something for me?''

''Anything, Em,'' he said in relief, hoping she was finally going to be reasonable as he sidestepped over Ernie's damp mop as the maintenance man swabbed the diner floor, dampening numerous sets of toes along the way. ''Anything at all.''

''Go home,'' she said firmly.

''Em,'' he said in exasperation, throwing up his hands.

''I'm serious, Joshua.'' Trying to ignore him, she stopped to refill the mayor's cup, giving him a warm smile.

''How you doing there, Emma girl?'' the mayor asked, lifting his cup in salute. ''Heard you were home. It's good to have you back.'' He took a sip of his coffee. ''Real good.''

She grinned. ''It's good to be home, Mayor.'' She moved to the next booth to check the breakfast setups for the monthly meeting of the Saddle Falls Quilting Club with Josh hot on her heels. ''Go home, Josh,'' she repeated through gritted teeth, flashing a smile to Kay Beckett, president of the quilting club who'd already arrived. "Or to work. Go somewhere... anywhere." Turning to him, she closed her eyes and prayed for patience. "And please stop following me and bothering me. I've got work to do."

"That's the whole point, Em. You shouldn't be working."

"Don't start, Joshua Ryan, please don't start this." Em turned to look at him over her shoulder. "Trust me, I am not in the mood for this again this morning."

"What are you in the mood for, Em?" he teased, trying to get her to lighten up and realizing he was on dangerous ground with her. "And speaking of food, did you even eat this morning?"

Not bothering to answer him, she merely gave him a scathing look, then continued on with her duties. He continued to sidestep next to her, talking all the while.

"Em, I'm just trying to be practical here. Maybe get you to look at a couple of other options."

"Josh, believe me, there are no other options."

"Yes, there are, Em. If you sold the diner you could invest the money and at least stay home until the baby's born."

"True," she admitted as she continued moving down the line of booths refilling coffee cups. "But then what do I do when the money from the sale of the diner runs out, Josh?" One brow rose in question as she turned to stare at him, waiting for an answer, coffeepot midair. "How do I support myself and my child, then?"

That gave him pause and Josh stood there for a moment, realizing she had a point. While the diner was a profitable business, the sale wouldn't bring in enough money to hold her for more than a couple of years—at best.

"That's what I thought," she said with a nod, moving again.

"Em, but think about this," he said, coming up behind her as she swung through the door that led to the kitchen. "If you continue to run the diner, you'll be on your feet for hours each day, lugging heavy trays of food, walking across slippery floors. What if you fall?" he challenged, darting around Ernie who'd begun swabbing the floor right between them.

"What if the sky falls?" she asked, knowing that anything he said was futile. She'd heard every argument he could come up with the past week and had rejected them all. She would do whatever was necessary to secure the future for her child.

Weary of his advice, yet touched beyond measure by his concern, Em leaned against the stainless steel food preparation table then crossed her arms across her breasts. She had to admit Josh had shown more caring and concern for her in the past week than Jack had in the past six years.

But then again she'd always known Josh was a special man. A man of character, confidence and absolutely total integrity. Three qualities Jack couldn't hope to spell, let alone exhibit.

"Josh, listen to me." Em turned to him, trying to hang on to her temper. She laid her hands to his wide chest, surprised at the strength she found there. "I appreciate your concern." She had to tilt her head up to meet his gaze. "Truly I do, but I have to deal with reality here and I can't base my actions on speculation or on something that *might* happen. I could fall walking in the house," she said with a careless shrug. "Or trip over a carpet. Or fall down the porch stairs.'' She moved around him to the large commercial refrigerator to pull out the necessary ingredients to make salads for the afternoon's lunch rush, carefully setting them on the stainless steel table. ''Or I could trip over your shoes,'' she pointed out, glancing up at him in time to see his smile. ''There are no guarantees in life, Josh.'' And no one knew that better than she. ''None. So I'm going to do the best I can to secure my baby's future and mine.'' She shrugged, reaching around him for the large set of wooden salad bowls stacked up so she could fill them as she chopped lettuce and vegetables.

Going to the refrigerator again, she pulled out the large wooden tray that held numerous heads of lettuce waiting to be readied for salads.

All right, so she had a point, Josh realized with a hint of annoyance, wondering when Em had decided to get so practical. But he had to admit, even if he didn't quite approve of what she planned to do, he had to admire her for it, wondering why Melanie hadn't fought so fiercely to protect *his* child. His admiration for Em was growing by leaps and bounds.

''Em,'' he said in a tone of voice that immediately told her he was not totally impressed with her reasoning. ''Do you really realize how serious this situation is?'' His worried gaze met hers. Those eyes, Em thought with a sigh, always had the ability to make her feel as if he could see right through her.

She glanced away, afraid he might see the fear that she held deep in her heart, a fear she couldn't and wouldn't admit to him or anyone else. Pride alone prevented it.

''Em?''

She whirled back to face him, her temper simmering, her eyes blazing. "You don't think I'm taking this seriously?" She slammed the tray holding the heads of lettuce onto the metal prep table, sending the lettuce bouncing in the air like yo-yos before storming up to Josh, poking a finger in his broad chest.

"Let me tell you something, Joshua Ryan." Eyes blazing, she stood on tiptoe to meet his gaze. "I've never taken anything *more* seriously in my life. I would never ever do anything to jeopardize my baby. Do you understand that? Nothing. This baby means more to me than anything in the entire world." Unconsciously, she pressed a protective hand to her belly. "If for one moment I thought what I was doing would harm my baby, then I'd stop. Immediately. But I'm not hurting my child, Josh. What I'm doing is trying to secure her future. And mine. To provide her with the kind of home, life and family, the kind of love and attention and affection I never had." Her voice hitched, humiliating her, and Em averted her gaze, not wanting him to see her tears, or know about the months of vicious emotional upheaval she'd just been through simply because she understood *fully* the seriousness of her situation.

And it scared her to death.

"Oh, Em, come here." Feeling guilty, Josh reached for her, pulling her trembling body into his arms. She was so close, the warmth of their bodies mingled. He could feel her slender body trembling against him and he wanted to swear again.

Take care of herself, indeed, he thought with a scowl, tightening his arms around her. Even with her pregnancy, he couldn't believe how thin and frail she was.

She'd always been so stubborn and proud, and she'd always tried to be so brave, but he knew her well enough to see beyond the facade she put on for the rest of the world. She was terrified right now, and was loathe to admit it to anyone, wanting to put up a brave, strong front. But he knew her better.

Josh frowned suddenly, aware that something was distracting him. That heavenly scent of hers—something sweet and smelling slightly of vanilla—was teasing his senses again, making him want to hold her tight in his arms forever and protect her from anything that might hurt her.

"I'm sorry," he whispered, his breath tickling her ear as he brushed her hair back from her face as if she were still a wayward twelve-year-old. "I didn't mean to upset you. I was just trying to be helpful."

The soft, honeyed tone of his voice shimmied over her, causing a warmth to unroll in her stomach. Pressed against him, encircled in his arms and the comfort of his warmth, her pulse kicked up, annoying her.

"Josh," she said, wiping her eyes and pulling back to look at him, a little off balance by her reaction to him. "Do you think you might try to be a little less helpful?" she asked, making him laugh.

Sniveling, she took the handkerchief he offered, then wiped her nose and her eyes, trying to figure out what the heck was going on, more rattled by her response to him than anything else.

This was Josh, her dearest friend, she shouldn't be responding to him like this. It totally unnerved her.

"Em, what am I going to do with you?" he asked softly, pressing his head against hers.

"Well, for starters you can stop following me

around before I trip over *your* feet,'' she said, making him laugh again. ''As far as I can tell that's the only real hazard around here right now.''

''You want me to leave, is that it?'' he asked, knowing this battle was lost. At least for the moment. That didn't mean he intended to give up the fight. And knowing her as well as he did only fueled his determination to do whatever was necessary to make things easier for her. He might not have been able to help or do anything to protect his own defenseless, unborn child, but he sure could do something to protect Em's.

Whether she liked it or not!

''Yep,'' she confirmed. ''The sooner the better.'' She glanced at the prep table filled with lettuce and vegetables that needed chopping. ''I've got things to do and I'd prefer to do them without carrying on a running argument with you.''

''Okay,'' he said with a sigh. ''I'll go for now. But I'll be back,'' he said with a grin as he headed toward the swinging door. ''For lunch.''

''Thanks for the warning, Josh,'' Em said with a laugh. ''I'll be sure to put down all the heavy equipment before then,'' she teased.

''How about a pizza from Angelo's tonight?'' he called over his shoulder.

''Angelo's?'' Her temper dashed, her interest perked up and she almost swooned. She hadn't had a pizza from Angelo's in almost six years. The thought of it now almost made her salivate. ''Deal,'' she returned with a smile, watching as Josh sailed out the front door, satisfied one problem was solved.

At least for the moment.

* * *

By the noon lunch hour rush, Em was certain almost everyone in town had come into the diner, demanding to be fed—immediately. She was grateful for all the days in her youth she'd worked in the diner. Once the lunch rush was over she was pretty much home free since the diner closed at three in the afternoon and didn't reopen until five the next morning.

"Hey, Em, can you come out here?" Aggie's voice filtered through the door separating the diner from the kitchen where she was still working chopping vegetables.

"Be right out," Em called, wiping her hands on her apron and swinging through the door.

"Heard the prettiest girl in town was back," Jake Ryan, Josh's oldest brother, said as he grabbed Em up and off her feet in a bear hug.

"Jake, oh Jake." Laughing, she hugged him back. "I'm so glad to see you."

While all the Ryans had hell-raising reputations growing up, none more so than Jake. Like his brothers, he had a fierce sense of pride, a strong sense of right and wrong, and an incredible right hook to back up his temper.

He'd given more than a few teachers and mothers a few moments of worry during his youth, but for all his hell-raising ways, Jake—like Josh—was one of the kindest, loving men she'd ever known.

And one of the most gorgeous, Em thought with a wicked grin, realizing that time had only added to Jake's looks. He was a bit taller than Josh, but not by much. And he had the same sleek black hair as all the other Ryans, but Jake, always the renegade, wore his hair longer than Josh's more conservative style. He also had the same incredibly gorgeous blue eyes,

eyes that saw far more than anyone would ever believe.

Jake set her down, grinning at her as his gaze went over her. "You're still pretty as ever, Em," he said with a shake of his head. He studied her carefully. "And a little bird tells me you're about to be a mother?"

"And I hear you're about to become a father," she retorted with a grin, watching as his face brightened and his eyes glowed. His joy over the expected birth of his child was so visible, so obvious it brought a pang of yearning to her heart.

"In just a few months," he admitted, climbing onto one of the stools at the counter. He shook his head. "Hard to believe, isn't it Em? We're going to be parents." He laughed. "Now that's a scary thought," he said with a shudder, eyeing the glass-covered plates behind the counter where the day's homemade pies and cakes sat. "Got any of your famous pecan pie left?"

"Got a fresh one in the kitchen, Jake." Still smiling, Em pushed through the door to the kitchen, cut Jake his pie and returned to pour him a fresh cup of coffee.

"How's business?" he asked between bites.

"Fabulous." Her eyes twinkled in amusement. "I think part is just curiosity about me being home."

He grinned, finishing off his pie. "Yeah, that and these fabulous cakes and pies, Em." He wiped his mouth on a napkin, then tossed it to the counter. "Listen, Em..." His voice trailed off and his face grew serious. "How you feeling?" he asked. "I mean, being pregnant and all, should you be on your feet all day? Working?" There was such concern in his voice, his eyes, she simply couldn't get annoyed at him, not when she knew that someone had put him up to this.

Josh again, she thought with a sigh, trying to curb her annoyance. He'd sent for reinforcements. Now he was rallying his brothers to his cause. Lord, what on earth was she going to do with that man?

"Now why do I have a feeling your brother sent you in here to talk some sense into me?" she asked, crossing her arms across her chest and looking at Jake in challenge.

"Me?" Flustered at being caught, Jake lifted his hands in the air as if to feign innocence, then shook his head. "Not me, Em. I'm innocent. Honest. I just dropped by to see an old friend."

Em knew how close the Ryan brothers were, knew how loyal they were to one another. She could stick needles in his nose and Jake would never admit Josh had sent him in to talk some sense into her, as Josh was fond of saying.

"Yeah, right," she said with a grin, deciding to let it go. No sense arguing with Jake. It was Josh she had to contend with. "Well, for whatever reason, I am glad you stopped in. And I'm looking forward to meeting your wife."

Jake wiggled his brow. "Yeah, you'll like Rebecca, she's a pistol."

Em laughed, knowing the woman would have to be a pistol in order to catch the infamous Jake Ryan.

Jake slid off the stool, tossed some bills onto the counter before raising his gaze to hers. "Listen, Em, if you need anything, anything at all, just give a holler, hear? Rebecca and I have been doing some traveling, checking out some tips about Jesse—"

"Have you learned anything?" she asked quietly, knowing how painful this subject was. Twenty years ago, five-year-old Jesse Ryan, the youngest of the Ryan brothers had been kidnapped from the family's ranch while in the care of his nanny. He'd never been found. Josh had told Em that Rebecca, a reporter, had written an in-depth article a few months ago about the Ryans and Jesse's disappearance, and as a result, new tips and clues had been pouring in. Jake and his wife had been checking each and every lead out.

"No, nothing, at least nothing to speak of," Jake admitted, rubbing a hand along his stubbled jaw. "But we're not about to give up. Someone out there has to know something. And I'm determined to find him. But for the next few months, at least until Rebecca has the baby, we're going to be home, so if you need anything, you just let us know."

"I will, Jake." Smiling, she cleared his plate and cup. "And thanks."

"Any time." He leaned across the counter to give her a big kiss on the cheek. "Take care of yourself, now, Em."

"I will, Jake," she said, watching as he walked toward the door whistling softly.

With a weary sigh, Em wiped off the counter, then went back into the kitchen to finish preparing the salads for the lunch rush. She was torn between annoyance and gratitude toward Josh for caring about her and her baby.

As she worked, Em thought about all those afternoons after school and weekends when she was in high school helping out her dad—resentfully at the time because she wanted to be with her friends instead. No, she mentally corrected as she placed the now full bowls of salad on the large round serving tray she'd been using to transfer food from the kitchen to the eating area—at the time what she'd wanted was to be with *Josh.*

But that was a long time ago, Em reminded herself as she swung through the door separating the kitchen from the diner. A long time ago, when she was very young, and very foolish, she thought, as she skirted by Ernie and his pail, juggling the tray of salads. Long before she knew how dangerous it was to fall in love with a man.

"Josh says you shouldn't be carrying heavy trays."

Em almost dropped the tray when she realized Ernie had spoken. Ernie, her dad's longtime maintenance man, rarely spoke to anyone.

"Well, I'll be," she muttered, still watching Ernie who continued mopping as if nothing unusual had happened.

Stunned, Em merely stood there for a moment, mouth open, staring after him, realizing whatever Josh had said to the man had to have been important enough for him to break his silence.

Josh again, Em thought with a scowl. Now he was talking about her to her employees beyond her back! Lord, what on earth was she going to do with that man?

"You'll be, what, Em?"

Her head whipped around. "You!" Annoyed all over again, Em glared at Josh and for the second time bobbled the large tray. She tried not to notice the way the custom-tailored gray pinstriped suit he wore fit him like a glove, emphasizing the broad width of his shoulders, his chest; or the yellow-and-gray paisley tie that only made his eyes seem wider, bluer. The white shirt was a stark contrast to the deep bronze of his tan, only making him look sinfully handsome, only annoying her further for noticing.

"Whoa, there, Em," he said, reaching out to steady her bobbling tray. "Here, let me take that for you." He started to reach for it, but she held on tight.

"Thank you, but I don't need any help," she said stiffly, pride preventing her from letting him take it from her. She held the tray tighter, her hands on one side, his on the other.

"Em, don't be silly. I'll take it. You shouldn't be carrying heavy things anyway."

"I'm not being silly," she snapped, unwilling to release her side of the tray and not caring that every eye in the diner was on her. This was a matter of pride. "And I'll carry anything I want," she said stubbornly, knowing she was being ridiculous.

He tightened his grip.

So did she.

"Joshua Ryan, I'm perfectly capable of carrying a tray, and doing anything else I feel like doing." Taking a step closer to him until she bumped the toes of his Italian loafers with the toes of her tennis shoes, Em glared up at him. "And if you say one word, one little syllable about my *condition*...I'm going to bop you with this tray!" she whispered fiercely.

"Okay, Em, whatever you say." Josh released the tray, overbalancing it on Em's side. It tilted backward, salad bowls shifted, then slid off the back of the tray, tumbling end over end, spraying Ernie's clean floor with lettuce, carrot sticks, radishes and assorted other vegetables and greens she'd just spent hours chopping.

Em merely stood there, mouth open gaping at the

mess accumulating on the floor. She turned for a moment to glare at Josh, aware that everyone in the diner was staring at her.

"Damnation," she muttered, sliding the tray onto the nearest empty table. She bent to begin cleaning up the mess before someone fell.

"Em, get up." Josh reached for her elbow. "You shouldn't be doing that. I'll clean that up."

Near tears, she shook his hand off, embarrassed that she'd let her emotions overrule her common sense. What on earth was wrong with her? She let her pride and her stubbornness get the best of her, and knew that the story of her tug-of-war with Josh would be all over town and then back by morning. Just what she needed, more gossip on top of everything else.

"I'll do it," she insisted firmly, waiting until the toes of Josh's Italian shoes were out of sight before continuing her clean up.

She felt a hand on her back and turned to see Ernie standing over her. A large broom and dustpan had replaced his mop and pail. With a grateful smile, Em wiped her hands on her apron and took Ernie's outstretched hand, standing up.

"Thanks, Ernie," she said softly, giving him a grateful pat on the shoulder. She turned to Josh. It was time to put a stop to this nonsense right now. "Can we talk for a minute?"

Em wiped her hands on her apron again, wishing she could push on her back to work out a kink, but knowing if she did, Josh would probably be on the phone to the hospital.

"Sure." Josh grabbed her hand. "Let's go outside." He frowned suddenly. Her cheeks were flushed and her eyes were blazing. "You can take a break can't you?"

"Since I'm the boss, I imagine I can." Still, she cast an eye out for Agnes, and saw the older woman nod her head in approval as she refilled a customer's coffee cup. With her hand still in Josh's, Em's chin lifted in determination as she let him lead her out the front door into the warm noonday sun, determined once and for all to set Joshua Ryan straight!

Chapter Four

Em gave a quick glance up and down Main Street to make sure that she and Josh weren't about to be seen or heard. She wasn't up to dealing with any further gossip about them on top of everything else.

Her feet were hurting and her back ached, but she'd die before she admitted any such thing to him. With a soft sigh, Em carefully leaned against the building, hoping to take some weight off her feet, nearly sagging in relief as her body aches immediately eased a bit.

After a full week of working, she was tired and sore, but she felt absolutely wonderful knowing she was accomplishing her objective. She was making her own way, securing a future for herself and her baby, without anyone's help. She was certain in the days and weeks and months ahead, things would only get better.

"How are you doing?" Josh finally asked, studying her face carefully.

''Fine, Josh, just fine.'' Her words were clipped as she worked to get her temper under control.

Cocking his head, he watched her. A slow grin tilted his lips and he lifted a finger to rub his brow. ''Ah, why do I have the feeling you're not exactly happy with me?''

''Josh, you had no right to talk to Ernie,'' she burst out. ''No right at all. Nor should you have sent Jake in to try to 'talk some sense' into me,'' she stated, repeating his own words to him and watching him flush a bit. Fists clenched, Em gave up trying to control her temper. ''Look, I know you're just trying to help, but you have to understand, I don't need your help. What you did undermined my authority and made me look foolish. You also embarrassed me, Josh, and made it look like I'm not mature enough or sensible enough to take care of myself or my child.''

That was the crux of it, she decided, the real point that had upset her so. The realization hadn't hit her until now, and now it had hot tears filling her eyes.

''Em, I'm sorry.'' Alarmed by her tears, Josh took a step closer. ''I never meant to... I didn't intend to... I just thought—''

''Josh.'' She laid a hand on his arm, intent on getting him to listen to her once and for all, to understand why she was doing what she was doing. ''Listen to me. I didn't come home merely to aggravate you—''

''I know that, Em—'' She held up her hand, unwilling to let this go.

''Please, let me finish. If I thought for a minute that I was doing something that would hurt me or the baby, I simply wouldn't do it. Honest,'' she added. ''I know that in the past I might have made some poor choices, and maybe my judgment wasn't right on target, and yes I know you frequently had to come to my rescue, bail me out of situations or protect me from something—even if it was myself—but that was then, this is now. I'm not the same person. I've changed, Josh, I've grown up.

And he was going to have to recognize it whether he wanted to or not!

"I know," he reluctantly admitted, dragging his hand through his hair with a sigh and wondering why he resented the fact that she had grown up. He really didn't need a reminder, he thought with a scowl. He was more than aware of it, remembering the way his body had responded to her since she'd come home. And remembering, too, the way that heavenly scent of hers kept playing havoc with his senses, nagging at him like a melody.

His reactions to her had totally confounded him, causing him to lie awake most of the night.

He'd come to the conclusion that he probably was more comfortable when Em was a sassy twelve-year-old and needed—wanted—his help and protection.

Needed him.

Josh sighed, realizing his pride was wounded because Em apparently didn't need him anymore, and he felt a bit useless to her. "But Em, I really don't think—"

"Josh." Her voice was stern as she took a step closer, her fists clenched in frustration. "I understand how you feel. But you're going to have to respect my wishes here. Please?" The pleading tone of her voice swayed him much more than her anger. "You embarrassed me, Josh."

He flushed guiltily. "Em, look, I'm sorry. I didn't realize—I don't know what's wrong with me." Josh blew out a breath, then glanced down at the sidewalk absently kicking a pebble with the toe of his shoe. "I guess just knowing that you're pregnant, knowing what you've gone through, well hell—" He broke off, unable to put into words what he was feeling, simply because he wasn't certain he *understood* what he was feeling.

It had been so long since he'd seen her, so long since she'd been a part of his life, that now that she was home, he was having to deal with and face up to a whole host of unfamiliar emotions—emotions he wasn't sure he understood.

And her pregnancy had only complicated things for him simply because she seemed so utterly vulnerable and alone, stirring up all the old protective instincts he'd always had where she was concerned.

He knew she was doing her best, struggling to take care of things on her own, and he admired her for it. Truly. It took a great deal of character, integrity and love to be able to do something so unselfish; to put your child's health and welfare ahead of your own.

After what her husband had done to her, it took guts for her to keep her baby, and to make a conscious decision to do whatever was necessary in order to keep her baby safe and bring it into the world.

Josh couldn't help it. He sighed, realizing how much courage and determination Em had. How much love she had to share, to give. Her actions touched him on a very deep level, a level that scared him in a way he hadn't been scared since Melanie.

Josh tried hard not to compare Em's actions with Melanie's, but it was next to impossible. Every action, every decision Em had made regarding her child was in direct contrast to the actions and decision Melanie had taken with his child.

His child.

It still hurt, he realized, absently lifting a hand to his chest where he could feel an actual physical pain in his heart. Even after all this time he still grieved for the child he'd lost; a child he'd never even had a chance to know or love.

Em had nothing and no one; no family to turn to; no husband to lean on; no financial fortune to rely on. Melanie had all of that and more. If she hadn't wanted him in the picture, Josh could have accepted that if it meant saving his child. Melanie would have had no trouble supporting or caring for a baby, not with the kind of familial and financial support she had. But what Mel *hadn't* wanted was to be burdened with a child.

His child.

"Josh." Concerned by his quietness, Em reached out and laid a hand on his chest, fearing she'd hurt his feelings. "Are you all right?"

She looked at him curiously, wondering what had shadowed his beautiful blue eyes. He looked as if he'd gone off somewhere inside himself, and wherever he'd gone had created such sadness in his eyes, his face, she wanted to just hug him, to hold him and comfort him as he had done for her so many times.

Shaking his thoughts away, Josh forced a smile, placing his hand over hers, enjoying the warmth of her touch.

"I'm fine, Em. Really," he added with a careless shrug when she looked like she didn't believe him. "Just an old memory." He shrugged again. "It's not important," he lied. "Not anymore."

He'd never told anyone about the baby; he couldn't. He was too ashamed. Ashamed that he'd believed himself to be in love with such a cold, heartless woman, ashamed that he'd been lied to and deceived, ashamed that he'd believed Melanie to be a woman of strength, character and integrity.

He'd been so wrong.

And his child had paid.

But he'd learned his lesson. Never again would he allow himself to let a woman slip past his defenses. Loving someone meant leaving yourself vulnerable to hurt, to devastation. He wouldn't ever allow that to happen to him again. No matter what.

"Em, look, I'm really sorry if I embarrassed you or undermined your authority. That wasn't my intention at all." He shrugged. "I was just trying to help."

"Oh, Josh." His words successfully defused her anger and she felt a well of emotion for him. "Thank you," she whispered, lifting a hand to his cheek. "I know you're just trying to help, but—"

"Em, look," he interrupted, dragging a hand through his hair in frustration before bringing his gaze back to hers. Their gazes met, held. "It's just...I care about you," he admitted softly, slipping his other hand around her waist, and smiling when he felt the slight bulge from the baby.

"I care about you, too, Josh, you know that, but caring doesn't give either of us the right to try to control the other person's life."

"Is that what I was doing?" he asked with a smile.

"Yep," she said with a smile of her own. "Afraid so."

Absently, he slid his other arm around her waist,

slowly drawing her close, needing to feel her warmth. "It's the lawyer in me, Em, I can't help myself."

"Try," she insisted, her voice light. "Otherwise I might need a lawyer to defend me for what I do to you."

He laughed, realizing how much he'd missed her sense of humor over the years. Missed her friendship, her trust, missed *her.*

"Em, I've missed you."

She had no idea why her heart was thudding so fast or recklessly. This was Josh, her best friend, he'd hugged her a thousand, no, probably a million times in her life, this time was certainly no different.

So why was her pulse accelerating and her heart leaping as if it was about to take flight? She'd put away her love for him at age twelve, when he'd made it clear he thought of her only as a friend, and a kid at that.

"I've missed you, too, Josh." In spite of her nerves, she forced herself to hold his gaze, telling herself she was being foolish, there was nothing to be nervous about. This was Josh. Must be her hormones acting up again. Relieved, Em forced herself to relax.

"I don't want anything to happen to you, Em, or the baby, that's all. You're all alone, and I just want to make sure you know that I'm here—always—for both of you. No matter what you need, Em, I'm here."

"Oh, Joshua," she said, as tears filled her eyes and a warm rush of gratitude filled her heart. No one else had ever cared about her or the baby. Nothing he said could have softened her heart more, but she should have expected it. Josh was and always had been the kindest, gentlest, most loving, giving man she'd ever known.

"You have no idea how much that means to me," she whispered, blinking away tears. "But nothing is going to happen to me or to my baby." She smiled at him, wanting to reassure him, then added just for good measure, "But I'm not so certain *you'll* be as safe if you keep interfering and running around town telling people to look after me like I was a wayward twelve-year-old."

Realizing how she must have felt, he managed a laugh. "Yeah, I can see where that might have been a tad...embarrassing." He looked sheepish. "So I went a bit overboard, I guess."

"Just a tad," she agreed with a smile. His hands felt so warm and comforting around her. Her feet hurt, her back ached, and more than anything else she just wanted to rest her head on his chest for a moment. Just for a moment. But it was a luxury she couldn't allow. She couldn't let her defenses down, not even with Josh.

Especially not with Josh.

"Will you promise me something, then?" Josh asked

"What?" she asked suspiciously, making him grin.

"That if you're not feeling well, you'll rest. Or go home. Or at least get off your feet?"

"I promise, Josh," she said solemnly, resisting the urge to roll her eyes again.

His brows drew together. "How's the morning sickness today? Any better?" He knew she'd been suffering terribly, which was why she was so thin. She couldn't eat, and when she did, she rarely kept anything down.

With a grin, she reached in the back pocket of her jeans and pulled out a wrapped saltine cracker, crumbled into pieces now.

"What's that?" Josh asked with a frown.

"That," she said, holding the cracker up like a prize between them. "Is a miracle. Doc Haggerty was in the diner recently. It was right about the time I was getting green around the gills." She grinned at the alarm on Josh's face. "He took one look at me, dug in the bread basket on his table, and pushed a cracker into my hand. Told me to eat it slowly with some warm ginger ale and it would eliminate the morning sickness."

"Did it?" Josh asked in surprise.

"Every last moment of it." Still amazed, Em shook her head. "I've got a whole pocketful of them. I'm never leaving home without them. They really work," she said, grinning. "And to think I've been suffering all these months for nothing." She put the cracker back in her pocket. "I made an appointment to go see him next week."

Doc Haggerty was a general practitioner and the only doctor in town, so he treated everyone for everything, and had delivered just about all the babies in town for the past thirty years.

"Good, good." Josh cocked his head to look at her. "So are we still on for tonight?"

"Tonight?" she repeated, frowning. All she wanted to do tonight was soak in a long, hot tub.

"A pizza from Angelo's? Remember?"

"Angelo's?" Her eyes glittered and she brightened suddenly. "Sausage and cheese. Extra large?" she asked hopefully, wondering if he'd remember their standard Friday evening dinner fare from their childhood.

They'd pick up a pizza on the way home from school on Fridays, then have a picnic on the Ryan ranch. They'd lay a blanket right in front of the little waterfall and creek that separated their houses.

"Absolutely." She was standing so close, he could feel the warmth of her body heat warming him. He could feel the slight swell of her belly as well. It filled him with both reverence and awe. "What time do you think you'll be through here?" he asked, trying to divert his attention from what he was feeling.

She frowned thoughtfully, trying to figure out everything she had to do. "I'm not sure. I'll call you when I get home."

"Okay. And you'll take it easy this afternoon?"

"Yes, sir," Em said with a laugh. "Promise."

"Em." Josh had no intention of kissing her. None. But something dangerous stirred his blood, making him move closer to her. "Em," he whispered again as he lowered his mouth to hers. It seemed so natural, so instinctive, he didn't have a chance to think about it.

He could only *feel.*

So many emotions, feelings, needs, desires. They all rose to the surface at once in a kaleidoscope that nearly blotted out the warning bells clanging in his head.

This was not the kiss of a friend, he realized, as Em's mouth softened beneath his, accepting his mouth, his kiss.

Her arms unconsciously snaked around Josh. Em was so stunned that every thought, every protest, she thought to utter fled from her head, replaced instead by a string of feelings so strong she felt as if the world tipped under her feet again.

But this time it had nothing to do with her condition.

Em moaned softly, then tightened her arms around Josh, tangling her fingers in the lush silk of his hair, savoring the softness. When he pulled her body closer until there was barely room for a breath between them. Em's sigh was half longing, half need.

"Em." He said only her name; that was all he was capable of as he set her away from him, visibly shaken by the feelings rampaging through him.

What on earth was the matter with him? This was Em. His best friend. His *pregnant* best friend. He had no business treating her like a...woman, kissing her like a...*woman.*

What was happening to him? he wondered, more frightened by his actions than he'd been in a long time. Em trusted him, as a friend should, and he never wanted to do anything to jeopardize that trust.

"I'll see you tonight." Anxious to get away so he could examine what had just happened in private, he gently touched a finger to her cheek, wanting to touch her again, just once, before he turned and walked away, leaving Em standing there stunned.

What on earth had just happened? Em wondered. She let her eyes close. She wasn't sure, but all she knew was that it had been wonderful.

"Hormones," she assured herself. "That's all it was. No sense getting alarmed." She wasn't attracted to Josh any longer. She wasn't interested in him any longer. She'd been over him for years. Besides, she couldn't afford to allow herself to be attracted or interested in *any* man. She wasn't about to forget the lesson she'd learned; she wasn't about to jeopardize her own future as well as the baby's by relying on or falling in love with a man. The idea was just ludicrous enough to make her smile.

"It was just hormones, Em," she said, satisfied she'd solved the mystery of why she'd responded to Josh's more-than-friendly kiss. "Just hormones," she repeated as she pulled open the diner door, prepared to forget the incident and go back to work.

By the time Em locked the door to the diner that evening, she was absolutely certain she could sleep for a month. She was utterly exhausted, her feet were burning as if they were on fire, her back was throbbing and she could barely keep her eyes open.

But, she thought, as she climbed into her car, she'd made it. Another day done and no doubt every day after would get better.

Certain of it, Em turned on the radio, humming along as she drove home, glancing around at the familiar, pretty little town where she'd grown up.

As she passed the Saddle Falls Park, she grinned remembering all the holiday barbecues and softball games the town had sponsored. Right next to it was the Saddle Falls High School where she and just about everyone else in town had attended. With the window open and the January air streaming through the car, Em smiled and waved at Sheriff Fitzpatrick as he climbed into his squad car.

It felt good to be home, she thought, flipping on her turn indicator. She finally felt as if she had a purpose in life, a reason to go on every day. She patted her belly. "You make it all worthwhile, Baby Cakes," she whispered with a smile.

Although she'd managed to tackle the everyday tasks of running the diner, there was still plenty to do before the baby came. She had to meet with her father's accountant and get a fix on the books and the bills. She also had to finally unpack her few meager belongings, something she'd neglected to do in the week since she'd been home simply because she was just too tired.

And then she had to think about redecorating the house. It was too dark and dismal right now. She wanted to make things light and bright, to erase the painful memories of her own childhood and recreate happier ones for herself and her child.

And then there was the nursery to consider, she thought with a grin as she abruptly pulled over to the curb in front of a meticulous two-story white frame house with a beautiful meandering porch.

But first, there was something she had to do right now.

She slipped out of the car, glanced around, then dashed across the street, praying Sheriff Fitzpatrick wasn't patrolling this particular street. Mrs. Richards, the house's owner, still had the most beautiful garden in town, Em thought, as she raced back to the car.

After glancing in her rearview mirror, she pulled into the street, then began humming along with the radio again. She'd have to start shopping—window shopping at least—for baby furniture. She wanted the nursery to be perfect—a welcoming place of warmth and love for her child. The mere thought filled her with such joy she was absolutely certain she could probably float home.

As she reached the top of her driveway, Em frowned. Dusk was settling in, bathing the area in long, brown shadows. But even from here, she could see there were lights on in the house.

Lights.

As if someone was in the house waiting to welcome her home. It gave her an odd feeling, one she'd never had before.

As she pulled the car to a stop, she glanced out the window again, then heaved a sigh of relief when she saw Josh's snazzy red sports car parked close to the house. Josh, she thought with a smile. Perfect.

He must have come over early. Absently, she touched a finger to her mouth, and would have sworn she could still feel the touch of his lips on hers. As far as kisses went, that one would rank right up there with the all-time greats, she realized. It was a good thing it was Josh who'd planted one on her. If she'd have had such an instantaneous female reaction to anyone else, she'd be heartily worried right now.

But Josh was a friend, and it was just a friendly kiss between friends, she thought, not wanting to give it any more credence than that. Certainly nothing for her to worry about. She wasn't about to lose her heart or her head. Not at this late stage, and certainly not with Josh. She'd learned her lesson once. And she wasn't about to read anything more into a friendly kiss between pals, certain he had probably forgotten about it by now.

Grabbing her purse, her uniform and the flowers she'd swiped from Mrs. Richards's garden, Em let herself out of the car and hurried up the porch steps.

Josh opened the door before she even got to it.

"Hi," he said, reaching for her uniform and her purse bundled in her hands.

"Hi yourself," she said with a smile, realizing how

glad she was to see him. It was nice coming home and having somewhere here, she thought. Very nice.

"Nice roses," he said with a lift of his brow. "Got a secret admirer I don't know about?" He ignored the streak of jealously that tore through him at the mere thought.

"Nope," she said with a grin, glancing up at him. "I stole them," she admitted shamelessly.

"Stole them?" With a lift of his brow, Josh merely stared at her, then his glance lowered to the roses. "Mrs. Richards's garden?"

"Yep," she admitted with a laugh.

"Em, you know if she catches you, she's going to call—"

"Josh, they're for you," she said, a bit embarrassed as she thrust the roses at him.

"For me?" Touched beyond measure, and totally confused since he'd never gotten flowers from a woman before, Josh's brow went up again, making her grin. "And exactly what on earth did I do to deserve roses?"

"Nothing," she said with a grin. Unable to resist, she stepped closer to lay a hand on his chest. "And everything," she added softly, only confusing him more. She had to swallow the lump in her throat in order to continue. She knew Josh was just being Josh, trying to look out for her and protect her, and she felt horrendously guilty about the way she'd treated him. She shouldn't have jumped all over him about Jake and Ernie; she should have just understood that it was going to take some time for Josh to get used to the fact that she was an adult now, fully capable of taking care of herself. Still, that didn't mean she had to be rude to him. "Josh, look I know I've been a bit..."

"Cranky?" he supplied helpfully, making her grin widen.

"Yeah, cranky and I've probably also been a bit..."

"Testy," he helpfully supplied again, his grin firmly in place.

"Yeah, that, too," she admitted with a grin of her own, dragging her hair out of her eyes.

Josh shrugged. "You're pregnant, Em, it's to be expected. I understand that pregnancy can play havoc with your emotions." He shrugged again. "I haven't taken anything personally."

"Good," she said in relief, realizing she couldn't let it go at that. For her own peace of mind, she had to apologize, had to let him know how much she appreciated him and everything he'd done. "Josh, I don't think I was being fair to you," she said. She blew out a breath, wanting to set things right between them. "Josh, you and I have been friends for as long as I can remember, and you know I care about you and would never do anything to hurt you."

"Em, I'd never do anything to hurt you, either," he said softly, his gaze going over her face. She looked exhausted. Exuberant, but exhausted, nonetheless. He couldn't help but feel a strong admiration for her. She was handling her situation with dignity and aplomb and he couldn't have been prouder of her.

"I know. It's just that I want you to know that I really do appreciate all of your concern and your help, even if I haven't exactly acted like it." She stepped closer. "It means a great deal to me Josh, especially now, in light of the circumstances." She laid a hand over her belly, before glancing up at him, a gloss of tears shimmering in her eyes. "Josh, I promise I'll try to stop feeling so defensive just because you're concerned about me and the baby.''

''Em?''

''What?'' She blinked up at him, then sniveled.

''Speaking of defensive.'' With a grin, he held up the roses. ''Since I've just accepted stolen property, that makes me an accessory after the fact. So when Sheriff Fitzpatrick arrests us, we're both going to need a defense attorney.''

She laughed, realizing Josh was telling her all was forgiven. ''Thanks, Josh.'' Relieved, she stood on tiptoe and kissed his cheek. The scent of his cologne infiltrated her senses, making her sigh.

She looked into his eyes and saw so many things she'd never seen in a man's eyes before, not even her husband's.

Kindness. Caring. Concern.

They moved her and made her feel more ashamed than ever for her behavior toward him, and more determined not to let her fear over letting a man get close to her override her common sense.

Again.

''I hope you don't mind, but I thought I'd just come straight here and get started,'' Josh said, shutting the door behind her. He headed toward the kitchen to put the roses in water.

''Get started?'' she repeated, crossing the room and dropping down onto the couch and lifting her sore, tired legs atop the coffee table. She glanced toward the kitchen, then sighed at the thought of all the work that needed to be done to get the house ready for the baby, to make it a real home, the kind she'd always wanted. ''Get started doing what?'' she called.

''Get started checking the house out and helping

you get it ready for the baby.'' Dressed in work jeans that had tiny little holes at the corner of the pockets and were worn white in several spots, along with a white T-shirt splattered here and there with paint, she was absolutely certain Josh had never looked more gorgeous.

Good thing they were just friends, she thought, eyeing him carefully. Or else she'd truly have a hard time not…jumping him.

''You're—you're going to help me?'' she asked in stunned surprise, remembering when she'd told him the other day that she wanted to fix up the house before the baby came.

Absently, he scratched his stubbled chin, his eyes twinkling. ''No, Em, I thought I'd stand by and watch you do it all by yourself. Jake and Jared offered to help as well.'' He ruffled her hair, then took a good look at her. ''Rough day?'' he asked, sitting next to her.

''No, just long.'' She grinned. ''I'll get used to it. It feels good to be doing something positive, Josh. Even if every bone and muscle in my body is screaming with fatigue.''

''Turn around,'' he instructed, turning her so that her back was to him. He began to massage her sore, aching shoulders and Em's eyes closed and she moaned in pleasure.

''Oh, Josh, that's positively sinful.''

He grinned. ''Feel good?''

''Better than good.'' She forced her eyes open. ''Keep this up and you can hire yourself out. Give up the paltry funds you make lawyering, and you could get rich hiring yourself out as a masseur.''

''Now there's a thought,'' he said, pretending to

give it serious consideration before moving his hands to the tight muscles in her neck.

"This is blissful," she said with a sigh, enjoying the touch of his hands on her skin. Her body.

Unable to speak, she merely let several little groans slip from her as he continued to work the tightness and the tension from her neck and shoulders.

"So...how's it going?" He was so close, she could feel his sweet, warm breath fan the back of her bare neck. It sent a shiver racing over her as well as an ache she couldn't quite get a handle on at the moment since she was far too distracted.

"Mmm, good," she murmured without turning around. "Really good. That is if you don't count the tray of salads I dropped—"

"Ah, not your fault, Em. I'd say that was interference," he said, admitting his part and massaging small circles into her lower neck,

"And then of course, this afternoon I accidentally dumped a bowl of chili on old man Weaver."

"Can't think of a better place for it," he admitted absently, fascinated by the silky skin at the nape of her neck.

She shook her head. The former principal of the Saddle Falls High School had always been a cranky curmudgeon. "How can that man still be such a crab? He was a crab when we were kids, and he's even worse now."

"Hey, at least he's good at *something,*" Josh murmured, still staring at the glorious skin on her neck.

He fought the urge to press his lips there, to see if the skin was as soft, as silky as it looked. "So, you think you're going to be able to handle things?" he asked, struggling to get his thoughts under control.

"Yep," she said confidently, letting out another soft moan when Josh's thumbs pressed on a particularly sore spot. "Definitely," she added more firmly, hoping he'd finally drop the idea of talking her into selling the diner.

"Em?"

"Hmm?" Eyes closed, she all but swayed against him. He was successfully rubbing all the day's kinks and cramps from her throbbing aching muscles.

"I'm sorry about the past week."

"Which part?" she asked with a laugh.

"Well, all of it, I guess."

She turned to him, her gaze soft. "Well, you're forgiven, Josh. But let's make a deal. I promise that if I need any help or if I'm not able to handle something, you'll be the first to know."

"And what's my part of the deal?" he asked suspiciously.

"You promise to try not to worry. To try to remember that I'm not twelve any longer, and if I need something or want something I'm old enough and smart enough to ask for help."

He thought about it for a moment. "Deal," he said, extending his hand.

She shook it, relieved. "Thanks, Josh." He continued to hold her hand, his skin soft, warm and comforting.

He glanced at his watch. "You've got just enough time to soak in a tub before the pizza gets here."

"A hot bath *and* a pizza?" She grinned, then let him help her to her feet and lead her down the hallway toward the master bedroom. Her hand fit perfectly in his, she realized. And it felt so comfortable, so natural. She caught a hint of something sweet and floral, then stopped, turning to him. "What is that heavenly smell?"

"Bubble bath," he said. He shifted his weight uncomfortably. "I—I remembered how you used to dream about taking long, luxurious bubble baths. So I stopped and picked some up some bubble bath for you on my way here. Martha Powers says this stuff has all the emollients your skin needs to keep it soft, especially during pregnancy." Looking into those gorgeous eyes of hers, he wasn't going to think about how soft her skin already was. And whether or not she was that soft all over. "And…and…" He was losing his train of thought, looking into her beautiful eyes.

"And…?" she asked with a lift of her brow, wondering why he was tongue-tied. Josh had never been shy or tongue-tied, at least not that she could ever remember.

Struggling to get back the thread of conversation, Josh averted his gaze to somewhere over her head. "And, she said that it has something in it to ease sore, aching muscles."

"So it's a miracle cure, is that what you're telling me?" Em laughed, touched beyond measure by his thoughtfulness and his kindness. "Is Martha still working at the pharmacy?"

"Yep. She's going to be there until they wheel her out," he said with a laugh, not adding that Martha had also asked him a gazillion questions about just who he was buying expensive bubble bath for. It would probably be all over town by morning.

"A massage, a pizza, and a bubble bath." Em shook her head, not wanting to tell Josh that these small things were absolute indulgent luxuries after the past few months.

As was having someone care about her and be concerned about her and her unborn child. Feeling touched, and more than a bit weepy, Em cursed her hormones. They were obviously acting up again.

Em sighed, banking down the sudden longing that tapped at her lonely heart. There was a time when Josh's attention would have warmed her scarred heart.

Now, it only frightened her because as much as she could tell herself Josh was just a friend, and only a friend, Em knew that what she told herself and controlling her emotions just might be too separate and distinct things.

Which was why she was suddenly so off balance and yes…frightened. But it was a different kind of fear than she'd faced these past few months when she'd been all alone and so terribly frightened.

Josh's kindness, his caring made her feel far too vulnerable right now. The past few months had left her so emotionally shaky, she wasn't certain she was even thinking clearly. All she knew—all she'd ever known—was that no matter what, she had to protect her baby.

And the only way she could do that was to make certain she never put her heart at risk again.

Not ever.

She couldn't allow her own emotions to blind her to reality. She'd done it once, and never wanted to go through that kind of devastation and pain again.

She knew Josh cared about her…as a friend. And only a friend, she told herself. He'd never, ever given her any indication he'd felt otherwise, and so for her to even be thinking about anything more was both ridiculous and dangerous.

"Thanks, Josh." She leaned on tiptoe and kissed his cheek again, then drew back slowly, his masculine scent so enticing it almost made her dizzy. She had an unbearable urge to just bury her face in his neck, to inhale that wonderful scent she'd always associated with Josh. Only with Josh. There was a comfort and security with him, perhaps because they knew each other so well, perhaps because she also knew he'd never hurt her.

"But if you keep this up, Josh, I'm going to get spoiled."

"Spoiled?" he repeated softly, reaching out to brush a strand of hair off her cheek, wanting—needing—to touch her. Just to assure himself she really was all right, he told himself. Pleased that he'd pleased her, he grinned. "Well, Em, I guess that's what friends are for."

Chapter Five

January and February's chill gave way to a mid-March that began to hint at spring. But by the end of March all hints of spring had vanished as summer temperatures bore down on the spring buds with wicked abandon, soaring the temperatures to close to ninety degrees during the day, with barely a cooldown at night, announcing the arrival of an early summer.

In spite of separate air-conditioning units that cranked almost night and day, Doc Haggerty's small medical office, located two doors down from the diner, was uncomfortably warm on this Saturday afternoon.

The waiting room was elbow to elbow with women in various stages of pregnancy all trying to find some relief from the heat. Apparently Saturday was expectant mother day, Josh thought, feeling a bit out of place.

Dressed in paint-splattered cutoffs and a torn T-shirt, Josh took one look at the assembled group and opted to pace the length of the reception area as he waited for Em. He felt ridiculous in his size fourteen tennis shoes pacing a path in a pastel-pink carpet that was decorated with tiny little baby booties and bottles.

"Joshua?" Hazel, Doc Haggerty's nurse glared at him over the top of her reading spectacles as he paced in front of her desk. Again.

"Yes, ma'am?"

"If you pace a hole in that carpet, I'm going to send your granddaddy the bill.'

He smothered a grin. Hazel had been with Doc Haggerty as long as anyone could remember. And since Doc Haggerty had delivered Josh and all of his brothers, he figured Hazel was old enough to speak her mind.

"Yes, ma'am." He hesitated, then leaned toward her. "But what the blazes is taking so long?" Josh glanced at his watch, then commented, "Em's been in there almost an hour."

"Babies take time, Joshua."

"But she's not having the baby now—" He broke off, his face drained of color and he stepped closer to Hazel's desk. "Is she?" His heart had jumped into double time and he could feel sweat dampen his palms.

"No, Joshua, I reckon she's not or one of us might have heard something about it by now." Hazel consulted a small card with Em's vital information on it. Josh tried to peek at the information on it and only earned another scowl from Hazel. "Let's see now, according to this, I imagine Em won't be having that baby for about six more weeks give or take a day or two."

"So then why has she been in there so long?" he asked, slipping his damp hands in his jeans pockets because he didn't know what else to do with them.

"Josh?" Smiling, Doc Haggerty stood in the open doorway of one of the examining rooms down the hall. "Can you come in here a moment?"

Josh didn't wait to be asked twice. He bolted around Hazel's desk and down the hallway. "What's wrong, Doc? What's taking so long? How's Em?"

Laughing, Doc Haggerty patted him on the back. "Josh, if you don't calm down before Em has this baby I'm going to have to put you on tranquilizers." He stopped Josh with a soft hand to his arm. "Josh, listen to me. Em's fine. Perfectly fine. She's a normal, healthy woman in the prime of her life, and I expect she's going to have a perfectly normal, uneventful pregnancy." Doc Haggerty's bushy brows drew slightly together and his hazel eyes twinkled. "But you've got to calm down, son. Between you and your brothers, Jake and Jared, I'm not certain who's worse." Both Jake and Jared's wives were also patients of Doc Haggerty's. "All this worrying is not good for you, Josh," the doc continued, "nor is it good for Em to see you like this. It might make her worry, and we wouldn't want that, would we?"

Flustered at the mere thought that he could be causing Em more stress made Josh realize he had to get a grip on himself. "It's...just...I've never—"

"Yes, I know," Doc Haggerty said with a laugh, pushing the examining room door wider. Josh could see Em lying on the table, a white sheet draped over her. "Like I told your brothers, the first time is the worst time, Josh. After this, childbirth will be a breeze. And it could be worse,'' the doctor whispered. ''Em could be the one having twins.''

Josh paled at the mere thought, wondering how on earth Jared and his wife were going to handle another set of twins. Before marrying Natalie, Jared had adopted a set of twin boys, Timmy and Terry, and although Josh adored them, he had to admit they were more than a handful.

''Hi, Josh,'' Em said, lifting her head and flashing him a huge grin. ''Did Doc Haggerty tell you?''

''Tell me what?'' he asked, stepping closer to her. Josh glanced around. He'd never been inside one of these examining rooms before and felt slightly out of place.

''I'm going to do an ultrasound of the baby, Josh.'' Doc Haggerty sat on a small stool next to Em. ''Em thought you'd like to see it.''

''An ultrasound?'' Josh repeated with a bit of a frown.

''It's a picture of the baby, Josh. In the womb.''

''You're kidding?'' His gaze went from the doc's to Em's to the machine that was now flashing a static picture like a black-and-white television out of focus.

''Nope. Not kidding at all, Josh. Just watch the monitor.'' Doc Haggerty pointed. ''See that moving image there, the one that looks like it's throbbing?''

Frowning, Josh narrowed his gaze and stared harder. ''Yeah, I see it.''

''Oh, Josh,'' Em's voice was soft and dreamy as she reached for Josh's hand and clung to it. ''That's Baby Cakes.''

Josh's stunned gaze went from the monitor to Em's face, which shone with joy, back to the monitor again.

''That's...that's...really the baby, Doc?'' he asked, his voice full of awe.

''Yep, it is, Josh.'' Doc Haggerty laughed then pointed at the screen with his finger. ''That's the head, Josh, and here, see these two long things that look like twigs? That's the baby's legs.'' Doc Haggerty scooted his stool closer. ''And from the looks of it, Em, Baby Cakes, is going to be a big one.'' Doc Haggerty grinned. ''I'm going to take a picture for you and Josh, Em. That way you can look at it all you want.''

Josh couldn't stop staring at the image in the monitor. Although blurry and a bit out of focus, he could just make out the outline of a baby.

Em's baby.

''Oh, Em,'' he said, nearly overcome with emotion. He'd never imagined, never thought until this moment about Baby Cakes being a real living human being. Oh, he knew it on a conscious level, but it was always some kind of abstract thing, off in the distance, until this very moment. Before Baby Cakes had not been a *real* person to him. But now...now...Josh shook his head, unable to comprehend the absolute enormity of the miracle before him.

''Isn't she beautiful?'' Em said with a sniffle, clinging to Josh's hand.

''Absolutely beautiful,'' Josh agreed softly, lifting Em's hands to his lips for a kiss. He couldn't stop staring at the image. It was so hard to believe that it was an actual picture of Baby Cakes, right at this moment, in Em's womb. The reality hit Josh like a sledgehammer and he glanced down at Em. ''She's as beautiful as her mother,'' Josh said quietly, letting his gaze meet Em's.

Something quiet and strong passed between them, simmered in the air for a moment, and then they clung to one another's hands and smiled.

"It's something, isn't it?" Doc Haggerty asked, turning to Josh.

"It's..." Josh paused, then shook his head. "I've never imagined anything like it. Never felt anything like it."

"It really hits home, the miracle of life, of birth," the doc said. "It's the most miraculous experience two people can ever go through together," he said softly. "Bringing a new life safely into this world.'

In spite of his joy, Josh felt an unaccountable stab of pain, thinking of another child, another baby who hadn't been so fortunate. The ache in his heart was so strong, so sharp, it felt as if someone had wedged a rusty knife there.

"Josh?" Em's voice was hushed and whisper soft. "Thank you for going through this with me." She had to swallow back the lump in her throat. Her heart was filled with so much emotion, so many feelings for the baby, for Josh. "Thank you for being here for me and Baby Cakes." Her smile was tremulous. "I can't think of anyone else I'd rather be sharing this with."

"Josh?" Doc Haggerty said.

"W-what?" He dragged his gaze reluctantly from Em's. "I'm sorry, Doc, I didn't hear you."

"Would you like to listen to the baby's heartbeat?"

Josh grinned, then glanced at Em. "Is it okay?"

She nodded, still holding on to his hand. "Oh, Josh, wait until you hear it. After seeing the picture and now—now actually hearing her little heartbeat..." Em's eyes swelled with tears again and she smiled at him, so grateful he was here to share this with her. She couldn't imagine having to do this alone, couldn't imagine how Jack could willingly walk away from this miracle they'd created. It was his loss, she thought firmly. His loss indeed.

"Hear, Josh, listen through the stethoscope." Doc Haggerty removed the instrument from around his neck, and place one rubberized end on Em's belly, the other ends he handed to Josh to place in his ears. Josh concentrated, then he heard it, the faint thump-thumping sound.

"I can hear it," he said with a grin. "I can hear her heart beating." He closed his eyes for a moment, just listening to the little life beating and growing inside of Em. It had been so hard to imagine, but now, seeing Baby Cakes's picture, hearing her heartbeat, she had suddenly become very real to him.

"Isn't it incredible?" Em asked, as Josh frowned. "What's wrong?" She gripped his hand harder.

"I don't know," Josh admitted, handing the stethoscope back to Doc Haggerty. "It sounds...different now."

Doc Haggerty listened for a moment, then grinned. "Hiccups," he said.

"Hiccups?" Both Em and Josh caroled in unison.

Doc Haggerty nodded, then chuckled. "The baby has the hiccups." He slung the stethoscope back around his neck and reached for Josh's hand, placing it on Em's belly. "Here, Josh, you can feel them."

Josh held his hand perfectly still, terrified of hurting Em or the baby and then he felt it, a slight blip in Em's belly. he couldn't help it, he laughed. "There it goes again." He glanced down at Em. "She's really got the hiccups." Instinctively, he gently began to rub

Em's belly in a slow, soothing motion. ''Easy, Baby Cakes,'' he whispered, causing Em and Doc Haggerty to exchange glances. ''Everything's fine, sweetheart,'' Josh cooed, continuing to rub Em's belly. He glanced up suddenly. ''It stopped.''

Doc Haggerty nodded. ''I'm not surprised. Babies are very sensitive, even in the womb. Although clinical research hasn't totally proven it, we believe that babies can sense stress, discomfort and all kinds of things the mother goes through. In addition, it's a known fact that if the baby's restless or has the hiccups, then soothing tones or soft music will calm her.''

Josh shook his head. ''That is unbelievable.''

''Most things about the birth process are,'' Doc Haggerty admitted, extending a hand to help Em sit up. ''The further along you get, Em, the more things you're going to be aware of. Pretty soon you'll start feeling the baby kick, particularly considering her size,'' he added. ''I imagine she's going to get a bit cranky being cramped in there. Now, I'm pleased with your weight and blood pressure, Em, but I have to admit I am a bit worried about how big the baby is already.''

''Is that a problem?'' Josh asked.

''Well, not a problem, per se, Josh, but I'll want to keep an eye on Em as she gets closer to delivery. If I think the baby's too big, we may have to do a C-section.''

Josh's eyes widened in alarm, but then he remembered what Doc Haggerty had said about not alarming Em. ''A C-section?'' he asked, knowing only it wasn't a normal delivery.

The doctor nodded. ''It's a perfectly normal delivery procedure, Josh. It's a lot less stressful on the baby and the mother when size is a factor in delivery."

"Is it...safe?" Josh asked worriedly, making the doctor smile.

"Very," he admitted.

"And...uh...have you done one of these before?" Josh wondered.

Trying to bank a smile, Doc Haggerty scratched his brow. "Well, Josh, I imagine in my thirty years of delivering babies I've done one or two—thousand," he added with a grin, noting the way Josh's shoulders slumped in relief. "But it's not something you should concern yourself with now. It's an option we have to leave open considering how big the baby is already and Em's relative size." He patted Em's hand, noting the worry in her eyes now. "We'll keep an eye on it, Em, and we still have time yet. A lot can happen in the last two to two and a half months."

Josh nodded. He'd try not to worry.

"Here, Josh, why don't you hang on to this for Em while she gets dressed?" Doc Haggerty handed him the small black-and-white photo of the baby and Josh stared at it again, unable to stop grinning.

As he let himself out of the room to give Em some privacy, he gently ran his finger over the baby's picture, his heart swelling with unbelievable emotion.

"Oh, Baby Cakes," he whispered. "You have no idea how much your mommy loves you. Or how much she wants you." He couldn't stop staring at the picture, feeling unaccountably connected to the helpless baby who was totally dependent on Em for every beat of her heart.

He also felt an unbelievable swell of pride in Em

for what she was doing; how she was handling herself and this pregnancy. With so many odds stacked against her, she'd never considered her own wants or needs, never considered what would be easiest on her. Instead, she always—always—put her baby's welfare ahead of her own.

Josh shook his head, wondering again why Melanie had been unable to love him or their child enough to do the same. He sighed, unwilling to let his own bad memories spoil this precious moment.

"Well, Baby Cakes," he said, walking back to the reception area with the picture cradled in his hand. "You are one lucky girl. And we're going to take very good care of you, your mom and me. Promise." He stopped in the hallway suddenly, wondering how and when it happened.

He wasn't certain, but he knew without a doubt, in one fraction of a second, when he wasn't looking, one adorable little baby had stolen his heart.

"Josh," Em hissed, grabbing his arm and nearly dragging him away from the approaching salesclerk. "I *cannot* afford that crib or the bureau or anything else they've got in this nursery." Tugging harder, she pulled him out of the decorated nursery room in the furniture warehouse.

After leaving Doc Haggerty's office, Josh had insisted they finally start window-shopping for baby furniture. She knew he was getting nervous because she hadn't even started the nursery yet, but she was trying to be practical. She was concentrating on saving money at the moment, not spending it.

"Afford?" Josh frowned, tugging her hand to take

her back to the nursery. "We're not buying, Em, you said so yourself. We're just...looking."

"Yes," she hissed again, giving in to a sigh as the grinning salesman approached, numerous dollar signs flashing in his eyes. "But I can't even afford to *look* at that set. It's far too expensive." And it nearly broke her heart. The display nursery was breathtaking, absolutely the ideal dream room any mother could ever have for their newborn, but she couldn't afford to spend more than she'd saved, especially right now.

She'd managed to tuck away quite a bit of money during the past few months, money that she hoped would tide her over in an emergency. With babies, you never knew what could pop up, and she wanted to be prepared for every eventuality.

"And don't forget Josh, I just ordered all that paint and wallpaper for the rest of the house, and have to pay for that when it comes on Friday." She wanted the house totally redone and ready before she actually had the baby. Since Josh and his brothers had offered to do the labor this weekend, she felt she could splurge and order some paint and wallpaper that she hoped would give the house a face-lift.

"Em," Josh said, scratching his brow, refusing to budge in spite of her nudging. "I told you before. I'll be more than happy to lend you the money for the nursery furniture." He shrugged. "I can afford it, and then you can pay me back...whenever." He knew she'd been concerned about money as well as getting the nursery ready, and he wanted to relieve her of at least one thing—if she'd just let him.

"Josh." Em closed her eyes with a sigh, trying not to lose her patience. She'd finally come to understand that Josh was not trying to undermine her, nor was he trying to interfere, he was just being…Josh. The wonderful person she'd always known, who'd been raised to help someone—anyone in need. Her gaze searched his face. "Look, I know you just want to help, and I appreciate it, I truly do, but Josh, you know I can't and won't take money from you." She softened her words with a smile. "Not now. Not ever." She'd been absolutely adamant about it since the day she'd returned home.

Josh rocked back on his heels and looked at her carefully. "Not even if it means Baby Cakes has to sleep in a dresser drawer?" The mere thought alarmed him. After what had happened in Doc Haggerty's office this morning, feeling the intense, immense connection he felt to Baby Cakes, Josh wanted to make sure she had anything and everything she could ever want or need.

"A dresser drawer?" Em laughed. "I think you're being just a bit melodramatic, Josh," she said, linking her arm through his and steering him out of reach of the salesman who was bearing down on them. "It's not that bad. And anyway, do you remember last Sunday when we helped Mrs. O'Connor set up for her garage sale?"

"Yeah," he said with a frown, letting Em lead him out of the store and into the bright afternoon sunlight. "What about it?" He fished in his pocket for his car keys, knowing he'd have to open the doors to let the car cool a bit before she got in. The temperatures had soared into the high nineties and he worried about her being out in the heat for too long.

"Well, she and I started talking about the baby. And she told me she had an antique cradle that had been her great-grandmother's."

Josh stopped. "Great-grandmother's?" he repeated with a frown, unlocking the car door for her. "Em, Mrs. O'Connor has to be..."

"She's eighty-two, Josh," Em supplied with a grin.

"Eighty-two?" Josh shook his head, calculating. "So that means the cradle had to be a couple of hundred years old."

"Yep." Em grinned. "And it's beautiful, Josh." She signed dreamily. "Just beautiful." She dragged herself from her thoughts and glanced up at him, surprised to find him watching her intently.

Whenever he looked at her like that, whenever she was the sole focus of his attention, it made her nervous and weak-kneed.

Deliberately averting his gaze, Em glanced back at the store entrance. "Anyway, she said since her children are all grown, and she has no family left, she'd like someone to be able to put it to good use."

Touched and delighted by the joy and excitement in her eyes, Josh stroked a hand down Em's nose. "So she's going to give it to you?" he said, pleased.

"No," Em corrected firmly. "She's not going to give it to me, although she offered."

Josh sighed. "Wait, let me guess, you're going to pay her for it?" he asked, his voice etching upward in surprise. Em could take this independent streak a tad too far, he decided, but thought better of saying that aloud.

She grinned. "Well, I'm actually not paying money, Josh, what we agreed to is a sort of...barter."

"A barter?" Cocking his head, he looked at her carefully. "And exactly what did you barter, Em?"

"Well," she began carefully, knowing he was probably just going to start worrying again. "Mrs.

O'Connor's going to lend the cradle to me for Baby Cakes, and what I'm going to do in exchange is take over the daily luncheon special to her for a few months."

"A few months?" he repeated, wondering how she thought she was going to manage this new chore along with everything else she was doing. He wanted to shake his head in frustration. He'd been trying to get Em to slow down and not do so much work, not add to her workload.

He had to admit that he did admire her ingenuity. Cocking his head, Josh looked at her thoughtfully. "And of course the fact that Mrs. O'Connor is all alone now and has a hard time getting around, and everyone in town worries about her has nothing to do with this deal you made with her, right, Em?" he asked, his eyes twinkling knowingly.

"Well, it's a fair deal, don't you think?" Em declared indignantly, flushing and furious that he'd seen right through her. "I mean, I need a cradle for the baby, Josh, and Mrs. O'Connor needs someone to look in on her, to make sure she's eating properly…and… What, Josh Ryan?" She wanted to whack him as she planted her hands on her hips and glared up at him. "What are you grinning about?"

Touched, without thought, he bent down and brushed his lips over hers, sliding his arm around her waist to pull her close. "You, Em, are something else." He kissed her again, setting off warning bells in his own ears. He was beginning to crave the taste of Em. Her scent. Her touch. Her…everything.

He was no longer certain that his feelings for her were all that friendly right now, but seemed to be edging toward something far deeper and definitely more dangerous. And it scared the hell out of him.

He'd been so busy protecting himself and his heart from other women for so long, that with Em, whom he considered merely a friend, he hadn't considered the fact that one day his feelings of friendship might grow into something more. He hadn't considered it, so he obviously hadn't protected himself from it.

Which might just have been a mistake, Josh realized now, watching Em and feeling something deep inside him stir.

Something he was certain he wasn't ready to acknowledge or handle. But still, it didn't take away this ache he had to hold Em, to touch her, to protect her.

Unable to resist, he bent his head and kissed her again, needing to taste her, to hold her close, to feel her pressed against him.

When had this need to touch her, to hold her, to protect her surface? he wondered.

And the baby, he thought absently touching the breast pocket of his T-shirt where he'd put the ultrasound picture Doc Haggerty had given him this morning. Baby Cakes, he thought again, wondering how one tiny little unborn child could have stolen his heart already.

Annoyed at himself and his own thoughts, Josh shook his head, took a step back and let his arms drop to his side. He couldn't think clearly with Em so close, with her wonderful scent teasing his senses.

Watching the sudden confusion he felt reflected in her eyes, Josh realized he'd better get a grip on his wayward thoughts before he scared Em. He was her friend, always had been, always would be. She trusted him, and until now had absolutely no reason not to and he wasn't about to ruin that friendship by entering a place Em had made very clear she was never going to go again.

He would never do anything to damage the trust they'd shared for so many years.

How many times had she reminded him that she didn't want or need a man in her life? How many times had she told him that she intended never to fall in love again, never intended to depend or trust another man again?

Not just for her sake, but for the baby's sake as well.

Glancing up at the sun, Josh decided it was just the afternoon heat that was frying his brain, making his mind travel to places it shouldn't be going.

Not now. Not ever.

Still, he glanced at Em, standing before him with her hand over her belly, her eyes wide in surprise, and he wanted nothing more than to pull her into his arms and hold her—forever.

He quickly channeled his thoughts in another direction, back to their conversation.

"That's a very kind thing to do, Em," he said quietly, struggling to get control of his emotions. "I'm sure Mrs. O'Connor appreciates it." It wasn't enough that she was taking care of herself and the baby by herself, now she was taking care of Saddle Falls's elderly.

He knew Em had always had a soft spot for Mrs. O'Connor and for anyone else who was alone and without a family to care for them. When they were in high school, Mrs. O'Connor had fallen and broken her ankle. Every day for almost two months, Em had gone over to the woman's house after school, checking on her, running errands for her, cooking for her. She'd even borrowed her father's truck to take Mrs. O'Connor to Doc Haggerty's to get her cast removed.

Em sighed, trying not to let on how her pulse was jumping or her heart thudding. Josh so carelessly touched and kissed her—in friendship, she knew, and nothing more. And of course, she reasoned, it was only natural since they spent so much time together.

Only natural for two friends.

Em wanted to scowl, realizing she was beginning to hate the word. *Friends.*

If she just thought of Josh as a friend, how come every time he touched her or kissed her, her knees grew weak and she wanted to cling to him, to hold him, to lean on him in a way she'd sworn she'd never, ever do again.

Feeling fearful, and a bit embarrassed that she'd made a fool of herself, Em decided to get some perspective on the situation, not to let on to Josh how much his touch, or his kiss was affecting her.

"Are you hungry?" she asked abruptly.

"Hungry?" He cocked his head to look at her. "Am I getting senile or didn't we just have lunch after we left Doc Haggerty's office?" he asked.

"Yeah," she said, letting her grin slide wider. "We did." She hesitated a moment, her grin growing wider. "And your point is..."

He laughed, relieved that his own tumultuous feelings apparently weren't effecting her—or her appetite. "Okay, what do you say we stop and pick up something to eat—"

"Double cheeseburgers and fries?" she asked hopefully and he nodded.

"Double cheeseburgers and fries it is. Then afterward, once it cools down—"

"If it cools down," she interrupted.

"Yeah, *if* it cools down, we can sit on your front porch and have ice cream?"

"Chocolate decadent fudge?" she asked with a lift of her brow, making him laugh.

"Is there any other kind?" Josh glanced back at the furniture warehouse, and a thought began bubbling in his mind. Em refused to take his help. She refused to take his money. But, she certainly wouldn't refuse a *gift?* A baby gift for Baby Cakes. Would she?

Chapter Six

"Em, here's one. Wilhelmina." Josh glanced over at her in the moonlight. The air had actually cooled enough for them to enjoy sitting outside.

"Wilhelmina?" Arching a brow, Em took a lick of her ice cream cone and looked at Josh skeptically. "You're kidding, right?" She studied his face. "Aren't you?" she asked weakly, making him grin.

"No, I'm not," he admitted. "What's wrong with Wilhelmina?" he asked, glancing up at her in the darkness. He was holding the book of baby names with one hand and finishing off the last of his cone with the other.

"I think," she said with a frown, concentrating on her ice cream, "that if we name the baby Wilhelmina, she'll have to go straight from the womb to the Supreme Court."

Josh laughed, shaking his head. "Guess that means you don't like it, then, huh?"

"Good guess." She took another lick of her cone,

then pushed the swing with her foot, setting it swaying.

"How on earth do you know it's a girl? You told Doc Haggerty you didn't want to know the sex and we sure couldn't tell from the ultrasound." His brows drew together. "At least I couldn't."

She grinned, patting her belly which seemed to be growing by inches every moment. "That's because I *already* know it, Josh. It's definitely a girl."

He sighed. They'd been having this same argument for weeks. He couldn't understand how she could be so sure, so positive. It confounded him. But then again, so many things about pregnant women—and women in general, did.

"Okay, then let's look at some more baby girls' names." He flipped a few pages, then tilted his head to see better under the porch light. "Here's one. How about Petingula?"

She laughed. "Josh, it's a baby, not a puppet."

"Guess you don't like that, either," he said, flipping to another page, and eyeing her, a teasing glint in his eyes. "Okay, this one's nice. How about Leticia?" He reached out and wiped a drip of ice cream off her bare thigh with his napkin. "That's different."

"I think we'll stick with something a bit more traditional," she said. She grabbed the baby book from his hand, tucking it under her thigh so he couldn't reach it.

"Traditional?" He grinned. He loved to tease her, to see her smile, to laugh, knowing she was relaxed and happy. It was such a change from the sad, somber Em who had come into his office on that morning a few months ago. "I'd say what you're going for is...boring."

"Boring?" she repeated, bopping him gently on the head with the little book before popping the last of her ice cream cone into her mouth. "If you had your way, the baby would have a moniker that would be the menace of her life." She rubbed her forehead. "You're going to give me a headache with all these unusual names." Grinning, she tucked the little book back under her thigh and out of his reach. "Josh," she said carefully, gathering her thoughts. She'd been trying to get up enough courage to bring this up for almost a week. "There's something I want to ask you," she said slowly, watching his face.

"Good, because I have a favor to ask of you, too, Em," he said.

"A favor?" She reached out and touched his arm. They were sitting so close, his thigh was brushing against hers on the swing, sending shooting sparks of awareness through her. "Josh, I'll do anything you want or give you anything you need, you know that. After all you've done for me the past few months..." She let her voice trail off. She couldn't even begin to thank him or repay him for all he'd done. "I'm so grateful—"

"Em." He blew out a breath, wondering why Em's *gratitude* annoyed him so much. Maybe because he wanted something more than gratitude from her, he thought, surprising himself. "There's no need to feel grateful," he said, struggling to keep his voice light. "It's just friends helping friends. You'd do the same for me if our situations were reversed."

"I'd do anything for you, Josh," she said softly. "Anything." And she meant it, knowing what she was feeling for Josh, what had begun growing in her heart was something far stronger, far more important and frightening than gratitude.

She'd struggled the past few weeks to contain the feelings that had been swamping her, feelings that frightened her and kept her awake and restless at night.

She hadn't been able to stop thinking about Josh's kisses. Hadn't stopped thinking about them or wanting them. More of them.

And felt heartily ashamed for her wanting.

She had no right to want or expect anything from Josh, she reminded herself. But that still hadn't stopped the flame of longing that had ignited the moment he'd kissed her, and kept growing day by day, kindness by kindness.

She knew she was being foolish; knew, too, that Josh was just being Josh, her best friend. But still, deep in the recesses of her scarred heart, she longed for it to be more.

And it was that longing that frightened her more than anything else.

"Em, I've got a friend who's had a little trouble and needs some help. He's had some bad breaks in life. His parents died, then he went to live with his grandmother and she passed away." Josh shrugged. "He went a little wild, got into some trouble, and well—"

"Josh, how old is this...friend of yours?" she asked suspiciously, trying not to grin, knowing Josh's penchant for helping people.

He looked sheepish. "Uh...sixteen, Em, next month I think."

"Sixteen," she said with a nod, understanding perfectly. "Now why do I have a feeling this is one of your wayward kids from the Saddle Falls Outreach Program?''

The Saddle Falls Outreach Program had originally been funded by the Ryan family. It was a shelter right on the outskirts of town that housed kids who'd been in trouble, had been abused or were simply runaways or at risk in some other way.

Working in conjunction with the county sheriff and the court system, the sprawling center was manned by several full-time social workers, as well as a physician who was on call twenty-four hours a day.

They not only housed the kids, but they also tried to help and rehabilitate them, insisting they go to school, work and become productive members of the community. They'd had a high degree of success, and even now, ten years after the center had been founded, they were still working to improve the lives of many youths and teens.

With funds coming in from the county tax rolls, just about everyone in the community pitched in and helped some way. But no family more than the Ryans.

''Are you still representing the center and doing legal work for them for free?''

''It's called pro bono work, Em.''

''So that means yes,'' she asked with a smile. ''Right?''

He sighed. ''Guilty as charged. Someone has to help these kids, Em.''

With a grin, she shook her head. ''And of course, Joshua, you think it should be *you?*'' she asked, feeling her admiration and her pride in him grow.

''Hey, Em, the way I look at it, everyone's got a responsibility to do what they can when they can. If everyone reaches out a hand, then, hey, maybe we'll all get where we're going and along the way maybe we can save some of these kids before they get in real trouble.''

Unbearably moved, she touched his cheek in the darkness. ''You know, Josh, you never cease to amaze me.''

''Why?'' He shrugged, slightly embarrassed. ''I'm not doing anything anyone else wouldn't have done. I just happen to have gotten there first, that's all.''

It was a lot more than that, and she knew it.

Josh was willingly going out of his way to try to help teenagers he had no relationship with or history with and make their lives better.

Her ex-husband wouldn't even take responsibility for his *own* child, she thought with a hint of sadness. How on earth could two men be so different? she wondered.

It was very hard not to compare Josh with her ex, and whenever she did, she realized once again what a poor judge of character she'd been.

''So, this sixteen-year-old friend of yours, *is* he one of your wayward kids?'' she asked, knowing the answer by the look on his face.

''In a manner of speaking,'' he hedged, trying not to grin.

Em sighed, then turned to him. ''Okay, fess up. Exactly in what manner *are* we speaking here?''

''Well, nothing really serious, Em.'' He paused, then said, ''Just a little...B and E.''

''Just a little B and E?'' She frowned, then realization hit. ''You mean breaking and entering?'' she asked, her voice edging upward in shock. He nodded and she groaned. ''Josh, how can it be a *little* B and E?''

He grinned. ''Because he got caught climbing in the little side window of Perry's Grocery. Actually, he got stuck. The sheriff was making his midnight rounds and caught him in the act. Hauled him out of the window into the police station, then called the Outreach Center, and they in turn called me.'' Josh shook his head. ''The kid was trembling in his boots.'' Josh laughed. ''For all his tough-guy facade, I think I scared the daylights out of him.''

''Josh, why on earth was he breaking into a food mart? That doesn't make sense. It's not like Jim Perry keeps a lot of cash in there, everyone in town knows that.''

''He wasn't looking for money, Em, he was looking for something to eat.''

''Oh, Josh, the poor kid.'' Her heart aching for the boy, Em pressed a hand to her belly, thinking about her own child, wondering if that could have been her fate if things had turned out differently. Just thinking about it sent a shiver over her.

Josh took her hand in his, holding it gently. ''His name's Sammy, Em, and he's really a good kid who's just had some bad breaks. Oh, he's got this real tough-guy facade like most sixteen-year-olds, but underneath it, he has a kind heart, as well as a conscience that tells him what's right and wrong. And I think if he has a little help, a role model or two, he might be able to turn his life around and become a productive member of society. What he needs right now is a part-time job after school, Em. That's one of the conditions for staying at the Outreach house. And I thought, well, since you and Mrs. O'Connor made that bartering deal, maybe you can hire Sammy to do your deliveries for you in the afternoon, and then maybe help out in the diner as well.'' And if she had help in the afternoons, maybe just maybe, she'd stop working a full day and come home in the afternoons and rest, Josh thought. Like he'd been nagging her to do for weeks.

She laughed. ''And you think a pregnant single mom is going to be some kind of role model for him?''

''Em, is that how you think of yourself?'' he asked softly, surprised. She turned away from him. ''Em?'' He touched her chin, tipping it up so she had no choice but to meet his gaze.

She had to swallow before she could answer him, tamping down the feelings and emotions Josh's touch, his kindness, his presence aroused.

She knew she couldn't even begin to start thinking of Josh as anything more than a friend. She couldn't afford to, not without disastrous consequences. She'd foolhardily fallen in love blindly before; she wasn't about to make that mistake again. Falling in love with any man was too dangerous. It made her lose her objectivity, and she wouldn't and couldn't risk it.

''It's not just how I see myself, Josh,'' she said with a careless shrug. ''It's what I am.''

''No, Em,'' he said softly, running his thumb over the soft skin of her chin, enjoying the surprise that leaped into her eyes. There was something else, too, he realized. A wariness. Why on earth would Em be wary about him? he wondered. ''You're so much more than that. You're a beautiful, kind, loving, responsible woman who's about to give birth to her first, much wanted, much loved child, and doing everything in her power to make sure she gives that baby everything it could possibly need, especially love, more than anything. I'd say that's one helluva role model for a young boy, Em."

"Oh, Josh." He touched her wounded heart in so many ways, she thought. Touched it and changed it, made it a little less scarred each time with his kindness, his goodness.

He was so close, and when he was touching her, like he was now, she had trouble thinking clearly. Right now, all she could think of was the pounding of her heart and the longing inside it.

She sighed, feeling slightly off-kilter by the feelings storming through her. "Okay, Josh. Send Sammy to see me tomorrow after school. I'll put him to work bussing tables and he can make the deliveries to Mrs. O'Connor, that way I'll be sure someone's checking on her every day."

Delighted, Josh surprised both of them by catching her up in a hug. "Em, thanks. I appreciate it." Realizing she was pressed against him from neck to waist, and he could feel the soft, lush feminine curves, Josh had to swallow hard, realizing having Em this close, having her sweet feminine scent tickling his nose was wreaking havoc on his senses—and his body.

Em might just be his friend, but she was still a woman—a gorgeous, desirable woman—and he was still a man. A man who still had all the normal needs and desires of any other man. With a sigh, he set her away from him, resting his brow against hers. "Thanks, Em. I knew I could count on you. You won't be sorry."

She laughed, her heart still sputtering from being held so close to him. "I certainly hope not."

"Okay, one problem solved, let's hear yours."

''Mine.'' She faltered, glancing away, feeling self-conscious all of a sudden.

''Come on, now, Em, it's not like you to be shy.'' Casually, he dropped an arm around her shoulder and pulled her closer. ''What's on your mind?''

At the moment, her mind had gone blank. It was very difficult to think clearly when Josh had his arm around her in that protective, loving way he had.

He was just being friendly, she told herself. There was no need to get rattled over it. But she had to swallow hard to give herself time to gather her scattered thoughts.

''Well, actually, there is something I'd like to ask you in keeping with the deal we made.'' With a sigh, she leaned against him, deciding she'd enjoy the comfort of his arm, his embrace. As long as she kept things in perspective, what was the harm? ''And I want you to feel free to say no. I mean, I don't want you to be obligated or anything—''

''Em?''

''What?''

''Just spit it out,'' he said with a grin, making her sigh.

''You know I have to register for Lamaze classes next week?''

''Yeah, that's what Doc Haggerty said at your last appointment,'' he replied with a frown, not entirely certain he knew what Lamaze classes were.

''Well, Josh, I also have to have a birthing coach.'' Tilting her head, she glanced up at him, wanting to see his expression, a bit worried about his reaction.

''Okay, fine.'' He frowned in the darkness, rubbing a hand over his chin thoughtfully. ''Em, what's a birthing coach?''

She blew out a breath. ''It's someone who is with you during labor and delivery, someone who coaches you on your breathing and helps you get through the transitions of labor.'' She hesitated. ''Usually it's your husband, but, it seems I'm short one husband.'' With a wan smile, she tilted her head to look at him, surprised to find him looking down at her, his face, his mouth only inches from hers. It rattled her again and she had to look away. ''And...well...I was wondering if you'd be interested in being my birthing coach.''

''Me?'' Stunned, Josh's eyes widened in delight. His heart leaped in excitement at the possibility of being part of her baby's birth. Baby Cakes had become real to him; a real little human person, someone he already loved. He thought his heart would burst with joy. ''You want *me* to be with you during the baby's birth? Em, are you serious?''

''Of course I'm serious, Josh. I can't do this by myself.'' She frowned. ''Well, I suppose I could, I mean other women have, but I think it would be a lot easier to have a coach than not.''

''Em, I'd love to.''

''Really?'' she said in surprise.

''I'm honored that you'd even consider me.'' He frowned suddenly. ''Em, what do I have to do, though? I mean I don't have any experience at this birthing coach stuff.''

''Josh.''

''I suppose I can check out some books at the library. I'm sure Ms. Wilson can find whatever books I need, and then I can read up on what I'm supposed to do, I mean we still have time,'' he added with a frown, mentally counting the number of weeks until Em was due.

"Josh." Em was trying to stifle a grin. He looked absolutely, utterly adorable. A little scared and overjoyed. She didn't think anything could scare Josh Ryan. Knowing that the prospect of helping her in childbirth had, tickled her to no end.

"You have another...what...four to six weeks to go, right?" He glanced at his watch, calculating time. "That should give me plenty of time to learn everything I need to know. Now what about equipment or supplies, do I need any special—"

"Joshua!" Em said with a laugh, taking his face in her hands to get him to stop talking. "Calm down. This isn't brain surgery—"

"No, it's far more important," he injected, so seriously she started to laugh. "Hey, what's so funny?" he asked.

"You." She couldn't help it, she laughed harder. "Josh, having a baby is the most natural thing in the world. You don't need to read up on anything. Nor will you need any special equipment or supplies. What you will need to do, though, if you don't mind, is attend classes with me. They'll teach you everything you need to know."

"Fine. When do we start?"

"Next week." She searched his face. "Josh, are you sure about this? I mean, I could probably find someone else if I need to—"

"Em." Gently, he laid his hand to her cheek, delighted when her eyes slid closed and she nestled her face against him for a moment. He wanted to sigh in pleasure at the longing tearing through him; a longing to touch her, to see her smile, to make her happy was growing stronger each and every day.

"Em?" He waited until she opened her eyes and smiled at him, a dreamy smile that warmed his heart.

"Yes, Josh?" she murmured. He was so close, she could see the laugh lines that bracketed his beautiful mouth, a mouth she'd longed for, dreamed about, thought about ever since the first afternoon when he'd kissed her.

She could see the warmth, the caring, the tenderness in his eyes and it made her heart ache with a longing that came from somewhere deep in her soul.

"I'm honored that you chose me, that you picked me to be your birthing coach. Truly," he said, using a finger to tenderly brush a curl from her temple. "I'm delighted that you want me to be part of Baby Cakes's birth and life. And I've never been more sure of anything in my life." Overjoyed, he pressed a light, quick kiss to her lips, felt hers tremble under his, felt the tug of desire deep and low. Unable to ignore it or resist, Josh groaned softly, then pulled Em closer, deepening the kiss, wanting more.

Holding Em, having her in his arms seemed to fill something inside him, something he had no idea was empty until that day he'd kissed her the first time.

A whimper of pleasure escaped Em, and she sighed deeply, allowing herself to relax against Josh, enjoying his touch, his kiss, his mouth. Wrapping her arms around him to bring him closer, she arched against him, curling her body closer to the warmth and comfort of his.

It had been so long since she'd felt such tenderness, such joy, such a feeling of being cared about, protected, cherished. She knew it was probably selfish and self-indulgent, but she was so weary right now, she wanted to just enjoy the simple act of kissing Josh—without worrying about the consequences.

Em sighed in contentment as Josh deepened the kiss, holding her tighter, letting his sweet tongue tease hers. She groaned softly, her mouth opening under his, accepting what he had to offer and giving back all that she felt in her heart.

Josh's hands roamed her back, the heat of his skin warming hers under the thin cotton maternity dress. Her breasts ached, her nipples hardened in response to his kiss, his touch.

A deep ache of need started somewhere low in her belly, making her moan as desire, hot and feral streaked through her, causing her breathing to quicken and her pulse to race.

She clung to him, wanting these wondrous feelings to go on forever. Moaning softly, she followed his lead, enjoying the sweet, wild sensations he'd aroused in her.

"Em." Josh dragged his mouth from hers, knowing if he didn't, then he wouldn't be able to stop at a mere kiss. Leaning his brow against hers, he sighed heavily, trying to get his breathing under control. He was shaken to his depths by the impact of kissing her, more so knowing that he wanted to do it again. And again. And for the life of him, he didn't feel one whit of guilt about it, only eager anticipation.

"Josh." Licking her trembling lips, Em lifted a shaky hand to his chest and felt his heart pounding as rapidly as hers. It scared her to know that he was as moved by the kiss they'd shared as she.

"We—we shouldn't be doing this." She wished

her voice sounded stronger. But she was so shaken by Josh's kiss, it was impossible to hide the effects.

"Doing what?" he murmured, still feeling drugged and a bit delirious.

"Kissing each other."

"Nonsense," Josh said firmly. "We're friends, Em. Best friends. We always have been. It's perfectly normal and natural for two close friends who care about each other to be affectionate with one another."

Perfectly normal? Em's brows knit and she looked at him as if he'd just announced he might fly. What she was feeling at the moment didn't resemble *normal* in any way, shape or form. What she was feeling was warm, wonderful and so scary she wasn't sure she could face it or deal with it at the moment.

"You think so?" she asked hopefully.

"Definitely," he said firmly, certain if he kept saying it, he could convince himself. "It's nothing to worry about, Em. You and I both know that it's nothing more than friendship, right?" He held his breath, waiting for her answer, knowing that at the moment what he was feeling for Em could hardly be classified as...friendly. No, what he was feeling was a bit deeper, darker and far scarier. But he wasn't about to admit that, not even to himself.

"Sure," she said, praying he wouldn't see through her lie. "It's just...friendship."

Relieved that she didn't see anything odd in what they'd just shared, Josh drew back with a smile. "See, so then if we both agree that this was just a friendly kiss between friends, then there's nothing to worry about."

Friendly kiss between friends? Absently, Em touched her lips and she stifled a laugh. She could still feel the pressure of Josh's lips on hers. Still taste him. If this was his idea of a friendly kiss, then she wasn't certain any woman would be able to withstand a *romantic* kiss from him. Not unless they wanted to die of pleasure. Then again, Em thought with an inward sigh, it probably wouldn't be a bad way to go.

"Now that that's settled, Em, I think what we need here is a celebration."

"And exactly what are we celebrating, Josh?" Not certain if she was grateful or sorry that he hadn't put any credence or special importance on the kiss they shared, Em forced herself to relax. She was merely overreacting, reading something into nothing. The kiss obviously meant nothing to Josh. Like he said, it was just a friendly kiss between friends. So why, she wondered, did that annoy her?

"Well, let's see." He slid his other arm around her, pulling her close so she was completely encircled by his arms. He rested his head atop hers. "We can celebrate Sammy getting a job. Or you finally getting some much needed help at the diner." He glanced down at her with a grin. "Or we can celebrate your new birthing coach."

She laughed. "Seems to me, Josh, that you're just looking for an excuse to do some celebrating."

"Yeah, I guess I am." He kissed her forehead. "So what do you say tomorrow night, instead of having dinner here, we have dinner at the hotel?"

She grinned, her spirits lifting at the thought of a night out. She couldn't remember when she'd been out to dinner last. "Josh, I haven't had dinner there since my senior prom."

"We still have the best food in town," he said with

a hint of pride. "So...then it's a date," he asked with a lift of his brow, making her frown.

"Josh," she said carefully. "I don't think pregnant women are allowed to...date." She'd never been on a date with Josh, and the mere thought was enough to send her nerves into spasms.

"This isn't really a date," he clarified, just to make certain there was no misunderstanding and not wanting to put any more importance on this than any other evening they'd spent together. "This is a celebration between two friends. Is that better?"

She let out a sigh of relief. "Much." She pressed a hand to her tummy. "Me and Baby Cakes are looking forward to our celebration, especially since I'm already hungry again or rather still hungry."

Josh laughed, tugging her to her feet. "So I've noticed," he said, still holding her hand in his. "Okay, I'll pick you up here at about five tomorrow, is that okay?"

"I don't know if I'll be home by then," she admitted with a frown.

"If you hire Sammy tomorrow, there's no reason for you not to be home, Em." He kissed her on the forehead. "Okay, five tomorrow it is." He bent and brushed his lips over hers once more. "Get some sleep," he ordered, taking the porch steps two at a time.

Sleep? Em thought as she leaned against the back door and watched him pull out the driveway. How on earth was she supposed to get any sleep when he kept kissing her like that?

Chapter Seven

Early the next morning, Jared Ryan walked into the Ryan family kitchen. Spotting Josh at the kitchen table, is head bent over an enormous stack of books, Jared frowned at his youngest brother. ''Josh?''

''Morning,'' Josh mumbled, stifling a yawn and rubbing the back of his neck.

Jared eyed his younger brother skeptically. ''Josh, it's barely 6:00 a.m. What on earth are you doing up? Or haven't you been to bed?''

''I'm reading,'' Josh said. ''And I haven't been to bed, yet. I called Ms. Wilson at home last night. She agreed to open the library for me so I could check out some books.'' Dragging a hand through his hair, Josh grinned. ''I told her it was a legal emergency.''

Jared lifted a finger to scratch his brow, trying not to show his amusement. ''I imagine Ms. Wilson was real pleased to be opening the library back up last night.'' Virginia Wilson had been the town librarian for as long as anyone could remember. She was as cranky as a sawhorse, and guarded those library books as if they were her children.

"So what are you reading?" Jared said mildly, heading for the coffeepot.

Josh leaned back in his chair, arched his back, stretched his arms over his head, then gave in to the yawn. "I'm reading books on childbirth." He bent his head and continued reading. "Jared," he said without looking up, missing his brother's look of amusement. "Did you know that there are three stages to labor?" His brows knit, and he jotted something down on the little notepad next to him.

"Yep, as a matter of fact I did," Jared said, leaning against the kitchen counter and trying not to frown. "What are you writing there?"

"A shopping list," Josh said, crossing out one item and adding another.

Jared moved across the room to peek at his brother's list. "And what may I ask is the list for?"

"Things we'll need for labor and delivery."

"Labor and delivery?" Jared repeated. He read the shopping list over Josh's shoulder. "A beach ball?" Jared said with a lift of his brow. He hesitated for just a moment. "Uh, Josh, what exactly do you think you're going to do with a beach ball during labor and delivery? This isn't exactly going to be a day at the beach you know," he added with an amused grin. "And I doubt very much if you're going to have time to play catch."

"What?" Lost in concentration, Josh looked up at his brother and blinked. "The beach ball? Oh, no, it's not for tossing, bro, it's to use during labor. If the mother rocks on it, then it can ease labor and help with transition."

"Josh?" Jared asked, waiting for his brother to look up at him.

"What?"

"Uh...is there something you want to tell me?"

"What?" Perplexed, Josh looked at his brother for a long moment. "No, why?"

"The childbirth books, the shopping list..." With a lift of his brow, Jared expressed a whole host of questions that didn't need words.

"Oh, I guess I forgot." Josh grinned, rubbing a hand across his stubbled jaw. "Last night Em asked me to be her childbirth coach."

With a nod and a smile, understanding came. "I get it now," Jared said, pouring himself a mug of coffee. He took a sip, noted Josh was looking at it longingly, and took pity on him, pouring a mug for him as well.

"Her childbirth coach," Jared said, setting the mug down in front of his brother and straddling a chair. "So, that means you'll be in the labor and delivery room with her when she gives birth."

"Yeah, I guess so." The thought, the awesomeness of the responsibility made Josh pale. With a shaky hand he sipped his coffee.

"Think you can handle it?" Jared asked casually. "Being a childbirth coach."

"I think so," Josh said, looking thoughtful. "I'm honored, truly, Jared, that she would ask me."

"Yeah, I can see how you would be." Jared looked at his younger brother carefully. "So, then what happens after the birth?" He sipped his coffee, trying to conceal his worry. He knew how Josh guarded his heart; knew, too, that Em was the one and only woman Josh had ever allowed into his heart. Josh had always claimed it was just as friends, but now, looking at his younger brother, Jared wasn't quite sure.

"After?" Josh shrugged. "The book says she'll probably be home within twenty-four to forty-eight hours—"

"Josh." Jared's tone of voice stopped him.

"What?"

Jared let out a sigh. "I mean once Em has the baby, you'll be her childbirth coach, I got that, and sure it's an honor, but what about when the baby comes home?" Jared fingered his coffee cup, knowing he was treading on dangerous ground. "Have you given any thought to what your role will be then?" Jared sniffed. "Listen, bro, I know how you feel about Em—hell, how we all feel about her. She's practically a member of the family." Jared hesitated, not certain how to go on. "But Josh, you have to realize that you're going to be instantly attached to that baby. You're going to fall so far in love with that kid—"

"I already am," Josh admitted, thinking about Baby Cakes.

"Yeah, well, what happens if in a year or two or five if Em decides to get married again?"

"Married!" Josh could feel the color drain from his face. He'd never thought, nor even considered that Em might get married again.

"Yeah, married," Jared said, softening his voice. "Em's a young, beautiful woman. You know how she's always felt about a family, how much she's always wanted a family. Do you really think she's going to want to spend the rest of her life as a single parent? And I can't believe she's not going to want more children. I mean, you guys are just friends and all, but eventually I'm sure Em's going to want a romantic relationship with a man. Marriage and a father for her baby.'' Jared paused, letting the full of his words sink in. ''And when that happens, Josh, where does that leave you?'' He could tell by the stunned look on his brother's face it wasn't something he'd even thought about. ''Look, you know I don't like sticking my nose in your business, but bro, I just don't want you to walk into something you're not fully prepared for.'' Jared shook his head. ''If you get too attached to her baby, and it happens so quickly, bro, you won't even know what hit you, it could be...a difficult situation for you.'' Jared cocked his head. ''See what I mean?''

''Yeah,'' Josh said, still stunned and reeling, Em involved with another guy? Married? Someone else loving Baby Cakes? Taking care of her? He didn't understand why the mere thought of any other man involved with Em or Baby Cakes sent a bullet of panic arcing through him. ''I see what you mean.''

''There you are,'' Natalie said from the doorway, her gaze taking in her husband. ''Jared, did you let the twins go outside to play before breakfast again?''

''Guilty,'' he said with a grin aimed at his wife. He held up his hands. ''It was self-defense, Nat, honest. They woke up full of mischief—as usual—'' he said with a sigh. ''And then one of them tossed Ruth's bone out the bedroom window.'' Jared grinned, knowing he loved every moment of mischief his boys got involved with. ''And then Ruth started jumping and barking. And then Ditka came chasing into the room, adding his two cents' worth of barking as well. The boys were jumping on their beds, laughing, and I figured if I didn't let them go out—all of them—'' he specified, ''mass chaos was going to rein.''

"And you found this unusual?" Natalie asked with a laugh and a shake of her head. "Chaos seems to be the rule of the day."

"Morning, Josh." She crossed the room to give her brother-in-law a kiss on the cheek. "You okay?" she asked with a frown when she saw the look on his face.

"Yeah." He forced a smile as he draped a free arm around her waist to give her a hug. "Just fine, Nat." He adored his sister-in-laws. Natalie as well as Rebecca. Each of his brothers had managed to find the one woman in the world that was perfect for them. And they were, he realized with a bit of envy, totally, blissfully happy, the kind of happiness he'd always longed for.

"Actually, Josh, I'm glad you're here. I talked to Rebecca yesterday and we were thinking about having a baby shower for Em, but I thought we'd better run it by you first."

Touched, his face brightened. "A baby shower?"

"Yeah." Natalie went to Jared, gave him a thorough good morning kiss. "I know she's had a hard time of it, Josh, and I don't imagine she has much in the way of baby things."

"Actually, she doesn't have anything," he admitted, remembering how she had longingly looked at the baby furniture in the display nursery yesterday.

"Great." Natalie beamed at him as Jared draped his arm around her to draw her close. "I thought we might have it at the diner, if you think that would be all right. I called Agnes yesterday to sort of feel her out about it and she was thrilled."

"Yeah, I think the diner would work. It's closed on Sundays, you could do it on a Sunday."

''Great. I figured since she's only got—what about four or six weeks—that we'd have it in about two weeks. Is that all right?''

Josh grinned broadly. ''That's great.'' He hesitated. ''Nat?''

''Yes, Josh?''

''Thanks,'' he said, standing up. ''I appreciate it and I know Em will, too.'' Quickly, he closed and gathered his books. Right now he needed some time alone to think about what Jared had said. ''Well, I gotta run. I've got to go to my apartment and shower and change before I go to work. He picked up his books and crossed the kitchen to kiss his sister-in-law goodbye. ''I'll see you all later. Tell Tommy I'll stop by tonight to see him.''

''Hey, Josh?'' Jared called, stopping him. ''See how Em would feel, about having a puppy for the baby.'' He grinned at his wife. ''Ditka's about to become a father.''

''Seems like everything is multiplying around here,'' Josh said with a grin.

''And you'll think about what I said, bro?'' Jared asked again.

Josh nodded, then went through the door, thinking of nothing else *but* Jared's words.

''Do you think he knows yet?'' Natalie asked with a contented smile.

''That he's in love with Emma?'' Jared laughed. ''Not anymore than I knew I was in love with you until I almost lost you.'' He bent his head and brushed his lips against hers, feeling a warm well of gratitude that he had finally woken up. He had no idea how he would have lived without her. ''But, I think I put the fear of God into him just a minute ago,'' Jared admitted, a twinkle of amusement in his eyes.

Natalie drew back to look at her husband, trying to look stern, but failing miserably. ''And what did you do, now, Jared Ryan?''

He laughed, then bent to nuzzle Natalie's neck. ''I just asked him if he thought about what would happen once the baby was born and he got attached, and then Em found someone else and got married...''

''Ouch,'' Natalie said with a shake of her head. ''That wasn't very nice.'' She laughed. ''Effective, but not nice.''

''Yeah, I imagine Josh is going to be doing some deep thinking and soul-searching. Jake and I, well, we've been worried about Josh the last few years. He's been a loner for too long. We just want him to be happy.''

''And you think Em's the one to make him happy?'' Natalie asked.

Jared laughed. ''Nat, we've all known forever that Em was the only one to make him happy. Let's hope he realizes it—before it's too late.''

With a grin of her saucy red lips, Agnes, Em's waitress, planted a hand on her hip. ''So that skinny little kid—''

''His name is Sammy,'' Em explained.

''Sammy's gonna be helping us out here in the afternoons.''

''Yes, Agnes, I thought we could use the extra help.''

''It's 'bout time,'' Agnes complained. ''Been telling you for weeks to hire someone so you can take some time off. You shouldn't be working these long hours now that your time is getting close.''

''Well, let's not go overboard,'' Em said, feeling a bit defensive as she glanced around the almost empty diner. The lunch rush was over and now, all that was left was the prep work for tomorrow.

''What? You gonna insult me by telling me you don't think I can handle things by myself?'' Agnes challenged with a toss of her head. ''Why, me and Ernie can handle this joint with our hands tied behind our backs. Ain't that right, Ernie?'' Agnes called as Ernie carefully mopped under a booth where a child had spilled his milk. Ernie didn't answer; he didn't even bother to glance up, but Agnes was used to Ernie's silences.

''I'm not worried about you handling things.'' Em sighed, leaning wearily against the spotless, stainless steel counter they used for food preparation. ''And to tell the truth, right now, the idea of having a few hours in the afternoon to myself to just rest or do nothing sounds like heaven.''

''Go home, then,'' Agnes said, adjusting the ties of his apron. ''Me and the new kid, we can handle things the rest of the day.'' Agnes's eyes glittered. ''And if not, well, there's always Ernie.'' She grinned when Em rolled her eyes. ''Besides,'' Agnes continued. ''Didn't you say you had some plans tonight?''

Em flushed. ''I'm just having dinner at the hotel with Josh.'' She shrugged, trying not to let on how delighted and anxious she was about tonight.

Agnes grinned, pleased. ''Well, take yourself off then, girl, and go buy yourself a new dress.''

Em glanced down at her frayed jeans and T-shirt covered by her white apron. She hadn't exactly had a lot of money for maternity clothes. She'd been making do with what she had, except for one pair of maternity jeans, which she'd practically worn out. "I don't need a new dress."

"Em, Em, Em," Agnes said with a shake of her head. "A woman never *needs* a new dress. For gosh sakes, what fun would that be? You should buy one just because."

Em laughed, unwilling to admit she'd been thinking about going shopping all day. "All right, I'll leave, but do you promise you and Ernie will remain...civil?" Even though Ernie never spoke to Agnes in front of anyone, Em had a feeling, just from the tension between them that a lot went on between them when no one was around.

Agnes grinned. "Don't you worry about a thing, Em. Me and Ernie will be just fine." She glanced over at Ernie and her face softened. "Just fine," she added with a smile, turning back to Em. "Promise. Now, get going. If you leave now, you'll probably have enough time to get yourself a new dress and take a nap."

Em fairly swooned. The idea of having the luxury of taking a nap in the middle of the afternoon sounded almost decadent. She glanced at her watch. "Okay, I'll go," she said, taking her apron off. "But promise me you'll call me if you need me."

"Sure, sure, sure," Agnes said without much conviction, taking Em by the elbow to steer her out the diner. "I'll call if anything comes up. Now just go. Have a good time tonight," she said as hustled Em to the door before she could protest. "Make sure you get some rest."

Em paused to give some last-minute instructions to

both Sammy and Ernie, then with a wave, she went sailing out the door, unwilling to admit how unbearably tired she really was.

When the doorbell rang, Em sat up, shook the sleep from her head, then blinked, more than a bit disoriented. When she glanced out her bedroom window and saw the sun, she realized it was still afternoon and grinned in relief, trying to contain her excitement. She glanced at the clock just as the doorbell chimed again.

"Oh, Lord," she muttered, scrambling out of bed. "I'm coming, I'm coming."

If Josh was an hour early she was going to strangle him. She'd been so exhausted after her shopping expedition in town, she'd come home and fallen into bed.

She'd set the alarm, certain she'd have plenty of time to shower and change before Josh picked her up. Now, the doorbell was ringing and she still wasn't dressed yet.

"I'm coming," she bellowed through gritted teeth as she grabbed her robe and threw it on. Hurrying to the back door, she stopped, pressed a hand to her pounding heart and took a deep breath before yanking it open. "Josh, you're early—"

"I've got an overnight letter for Emma Bowen." It wasn't Josh, but an obviously hot and harassed deliveryman. "I need your signature." He thrust a clipboard toward her, indicating where she should sign. Relieved that it wasn't Josh, Em took the pen, quickly scribbled her name, then accepted delivery of the letter without giving it a second thought. "Thank you," she said, before shutting the door and setting the letter on a table. She had less than an hour to shower and change before Josh got here. And if she didn't hurry, she was going to be late.

The letter forgotten, on her way to the shower Em stopped to look at her new dress she'd left hanging on the closet door.

Gently, she ran her finger over the beautiful cotton fabric. She really hadn't planned on buying anything, but she'd stopped into Ruth's Maternity Emporium, and Ruth O'Brien, the owner whom she'd known her whole life, had insisted she try it on. The dress was casual enough to be comfortable, but dressy enough for dinner in town Ruth had assured her.

The moment she'd tried it on, Em knew she had to have it. It was one of the most beautiful dresses she'd ever owned. Normally, she wouldn't consider lemon yellow. It wasn't her best color, but something about this dress and the shade of yellow did something to her skin, making it glow. With the short-capped sleeves, and empire bodice, the dress fit her perfectly, emphasizing her small breasts and her long legs. Because it was the new, longer length, it also seemed to give her petite frame added height.

Delighted, she'd purchased it, trying not to feel guilty. While Ruth was wrapping her dress, Emma had run next door to the shoe store and found a matching pair of yellow ballerina flats. Now, she couldn't wait to put them on. Humming to herself, Em stepped in the shower, her excitement building.

"I'm not going to feel guilty about spending the money," she muttered to herself as she washed her hair. She'd been taking a small salary every week, but banking all of it, except what she needed for absolute necessities. Never again would she allow herself or her baby to be at the mercy of a man. Never again would she be penniless and without resources with no one or nowhere to turn.

Sighing, Em shut off the water and stepped out of the shower, feeling better about her situation than she had in months. She had money in the bank, the diner was going well, and she was handling things. Em grinned. Quite a change from the day she'd arrived in Saddle Falls, exhausted from worry, sick with grief and fear, and not certain how on earth she was going to do what she needed to do to provide for herself and Baby Cakes.

"But we did it, sweetie," Em said, plugging in her hair dryer, and glancing down at her belly. "With a little help from our friends," she added, thinking about Josh.

He had been so wonderful and so supportive the past few months. Once he got over his initial fear that she was some helpless, hapless female off on another wild-goose chase.

She knew he still worried about her, and she loved him for it. Em froze with the hair dryer in midair.

Loved him for it.

The words reverberated in her mind over and over again. Her eyes slid closed and she laid her dryer on the countertop.

She wasn't in love with Josh, she told herself firmly. She simply couldn't even entertain such a ridiculous idea. She would never be so foolish, not again.

He was just a friend, a good friend, and of course she would have strong feelings for him, especially considering all he'd done for her the past few months. She'd come to value and depend on his companionship, his kindness, his ability to make her laugh no matter what the problem.

But she wasn't in love with him.

What she was feeling was merely gratitude, gratitude because he'd been so kind, so supportive, so wonderful, she thought with a dreamy sigh.

But he was *just* a friend, she repeated to herself firmly. And she was *not* in love with him. With determination, Em quickly dried her hair, then applied a hint of makeup before slipping into her new dress and shoes.

Feeling like Cinderella going to the ball, Em paced the length of the living room, trying to calm her own disquieting thoughts. When the doorbell rang again, she sighed with relief, then went to open it.

"Em." Josh stood there with a grin on his face, letting his gaze travel over. "You look beautiful." It was the only word to describe her. "Just...beautiful." Nervous, and not certain why, he handed her the bouquet of roses he'd brought her.

Touched, Em laughed suddenly, cursing her own silliness. This was Josh, there was no reason for her to be so worried. They were just...friends.

"Roses?" she said with a lift of her brow. "Mrs. Richards is gonna have your hide, Josh." She turned to get a vase for them.

"Hey, I didn't steal those, Em," he protested, coming up behind her and slipping his arms around her waist. "I bought them." He pressed his nose to her hair, inhaling the wonderful scent of her.

Aware that his arms were around her, and her heart was pounding, Em struggled not to shake as she filled the vase with water and set it on the kitchen counter.

"Thank you, Josh," she said quietly, giving in and

allowing herself to lean into him—for just a moment—she told herself. Just for a moment. ‘‘They’re beautiful.’’

‘‘And so are you,’’ he whispered, his breath tickling the back of her ear, sending shivers of awareness through her. He hadn’t been able to stop thinking about what his brother Jared had said this morning, hadn’t been able to curb the panic that occurred every time he thought of Em and Baby Cakes with another man.

The day seemed to drag until he could see Em, could put his arms around her, hold her, touch her, know she was safe.

‘‘Thank you.’’ Her voice as well as her body were trembling in response to Josh’s closeness, his touch.

I am not in love with him, she insisted, repeating the phrase over and over in her mind like a mantra in spite of the fact that Josh’s presence, his touch filled her with a need and longing no one else ever had.

I am not in love with him.

At least she hoped not!

Chapter Eight

Em sighed in near contentment as she pushed her dessert plate away and glanced around the glorious, gorgeous restaurant atop the Saddle Falls Hotel, providing a panoramic view of the entire town as well as the Charleston Mountains in the distance.

Their white linen-topped table, adorned with beautiful crystal candles flickering softly, was set right in the corner of the restaurant with floor-to-ceiling windows on each side of it. It was, quite clearly, the best table in the house.

"I feel like I'm going to have to walk ten miles to walk off this dinner," she said with a smile, resting a hand on her belly where Baby Cakes had been doing somersaults all evening.

"You enjoyed it?" Josh asked, taking a sip of his wine, unable to take his eyes off of her.

"What was not to enjoy?" she said with a laugh, closing her eyes and mentally savoring every single morsel all over again. "I think the appetizer tray was my favorite.'' She frowned a bit. ''No, maybe it was that salad.'' She rolled her eyes. ''No, actually I think it was the filet.''

''It was a fantastic meal, Josh.'' She smiled at him, reaching across the table to touch his hand. Electricity sparked, then hummed between them. ''Thank you.''

''You're very welcome.'' He linked his fingers through hers, turning her hand palm up so it rested in his, giving in to the need he'd had all evening to touch her. ''You look beautiful, Em.'' He sipped his wine again to moisten his dry mouth. ''New dress?''

With a nod, she laughed. ''I went to Ruth's Maternity Emporium this afternoon and splurged. I had no intention of buying anything, but...'' Her voice trailed off and she remembered the look on Josh's face when she opened the door. She was absolutely certain she'd heard his jaw hit the ground.

''Well, I'm glad you bought it.'' His gaze shifted over her slowly. She'd done something different to her dark, curly hair. It was pushed off and away from her face in some sophisticated style that only emphasized her elegant face and her huge eyes, which tonight were smudged with some dark-colored makeup, making her look both sexy and mysterious.

She'd painted her lips with something pink and moist and incredibly sexy. He'd had a very hard time not leaning across the table and tasting her again—just to remind himself that she tasted as good as she looked.

''So you've told me,'' she said with a laugh, flushing a bit. ''Several times.'' Pleased now that she'd splurged on the dress, she reached for her ginger ale, taking a small sip.

"You okay?" he asked, nodding toward her glass. "Any more morning sickness?"

"No," she said with a grateful smile. "I'm just thirsty."

Josh toyed with his wineglass. "So tell me, how'd it go with Sammy?"

Em laughed. "Great. I think things will work out well. He took the first delivery over to Mrs. O'Connor's this afternoon."

"So when will you be getting the cradle?"

Em shrugged. "I told her you and your brothers were going to start painting and wallpapering this weekend so I thought I'd wait until after you were done to pick it up."

"Sounds like a plan." Using his thumb, Josh caressed her hand. "Em, I did some reading last night."

One brow lifted. "Reading? When did you have time, Josh? You didn't leave my house until after ten."

"I had some time," he hedged, not wanting to admit that he'd been up all night. "I made a list of things we're going to need for the labor and delivery."

She laughed, touched. "Josh, were you reading about childbirth?"

"Of course," he said a bit defensively, wondering why everyone was so surprised. "I never go into anything without being totally prepared." Smiling, he shrugged. "It's probably the lawyer in me."

"Probably." She hesitated a moment. She should have expected Josh to not only take his role seriously, but to fully prepare for it on every level. He was so dear she just wanted to hug him. "So tell me, exactly what's on this list?"

"Well," he said with a frown. "Gatorade—"

"Planning on getting thirsty?" she teased.

"No, it's not for me. It's for you. During labor. It can get very intensive, you'll be using a lot of energy, so Gatorade not only helps keep your mouth moist, but also helps with your energy. Small sips only," he added, making her laugh again. "We'll also need Popsicles and apple juice." His brows drew together in thought. "I also added a small cooler to the list so we can keep everything cold."

"I see," she said, her eyes twinkling in amusement. "I'm impressed, Josh." She leaned forward, watching him. The scent of her perfume—sweet and slightly sensual at the same time—faintly tickled his nostrils, making him wonder if she smelled like that all over. Deliberately, he schooled his thoughts in another direction.

"We'll also need to get a large beach ball—" He held up his hand the moment she opened her mouth. He'd learned his lesson about the beach ball already today. "It's not to play with, Em," he explained. "It's for you to rock on when the contractions get intense. It will also help ease the transitions between the different stages of labor."

With a laugh, Em shook her head. "Josh, you never fail to surprise me."

"Why?"

Her gaze softened on his, tracing the lines of his beautiful face. "Because," she said softly, giving his hand a gentle squeeze. "You just jump right in with both feet, making sure you're totally prepared and ready for every eventuality."

He shrugged. "I thought that was my job. As your childbirth coach, it's my responsibility to handle all the things you need in order to make the birth process as easy as possible for you and the baby.''

''Oh, Josh.'' Em glanced down at the table, at their entwined hands, realizing how wonderful they fit together. She lifted her gaze again, her heart full to almost overflowing. ''I don't know how to thank you,'' she began softly. ''Or to tell you how much I appreciate everything you've done for me the past few months.'' At a loss for words, Em shook her head. ''I am so grateful for the companionship, the help and the support you've given to me since I returned to town, Josh, being there for me no matter what.'' Her gaze met his, then held. ''I'm so grateful, Josh, I don't even know how to begin to thank you.''

''Em.'' He hesitated, wondering why he felt annoyed at her *gratitude.* ''I haven't done anything more than any other man wouldn't have done.''

''Ah, well, I happen to disagree.'' She hesitated, thinking about her ex-husband. ''Josh, you know you're going to make a fabulous father.'' Cocking her head, she studied him. ''So how come you never took the plunge like Jake or Jared?'' She grinned. ''How come you never got married?'' She glanced down. ''The day I came home, in your office you gave me some nonsense about being too busy with your practice, the hotel and handling the family businesses, but Jared has the responsibility of running the ranch and he's made time for a family. Jake has a great deal of responsibility as well, but he's made time for a wife, and now a baby on the way, too.'' She raised her gaze to his. ''So how come you haven't made the time?''

Josh blew out a breath, glanced around nervously, then brought his gaze back to hers. ''I almost got married,'' he admitted with a sigh. ''It was during my last year in law school.''

Surprised, Em sipped her soft drink, noting the dark shadow of pain that had leaped into his eyes. ''What happened, Josh?'' she asked softly.

He shrugged. ''It...didn't work out.'' He wasn't sure he could talk about Melanie with Em. Wasn't sure he wanted to admit what a fool he'd been.

''Josh?''

He glanced at her and the look in his eyes made her heart ache.

''Will you tell me about it?'' she asked softly, reaching for his hand, holding it tightly. ''Please?''

He shrugged. ''Not much to tell, I guess.'' Stalling, trying to get his thoughts together, he sipped the last of his wine. ''Melanie was a law student, too. She was a year behind me. She came from a very wealthy East Coast family, three generations of lawyers and legislators. Being a successful lawyer was very important to her.''

''More important than you?'' Em asked quietly.

''Apparently,'' he said with a sigh. ''About six months after we started dating, Melanie discovered she was pregnant. I was overjoyed. You know how I feel about kids—family.'' Hesitating, he blew out a breath, then brought his gaze back to hers. ''I asked her to marry me. She asked for a few days to think about it. Obviously neither of us had planned on having a child, especially then, but it happened and I couldn't have been happier about it.''

''But she wasn't?'' Em asked softly, holding his hand tighter. She couldn't imagine a woman not being thrilled about having a baby with the man she loved.

Nor could she imagine any woman not wanting Josh or his child.

"No." He had to stop for a moment before he continued. "She went home to New York to see her family. I stayed behind because she needed some time alone to think things through. While she was gone, I did some thinking as well. Although we obviously hadn't planned on having a child while we were both still in school, I knew without a doubt that I could support both Melanie and the baby quite handsomely. And I knew that we'd have nothing but support from Tommy and the rest of the family." He shrugged. "And, I thought I loved her." He snorted in disgust, then shook his head. "I didn't even know her."

Something dark and haunting flashed across his face, almost making Em shiver. She'd never seen that look in his eyes before.

"Josh, what happened?" she prompted softly, caressing his hand in comfort, wanting to repay him with the same comfort he'd been giving her all these months.

He lifted his gaze to hers; his expression cool and blank. It sent a shiver through Em. "Melanie never returned from New York. I received a letter from her telling me that neither a baby nor marriage were in her future. She had a brilliant law career ahead of her and she'd worked too hard for too long to give it all up now."

Em's gaze widened. "Josh," she whispered, with a sick, sinking feeling in her heart. "The baby?"

Shaking his head, he blew out a breath. "She...got rid of it."

"Oh, God, Josh." Em's eyes filled with tears and

she clutched his hand tighter, wanting to ease the pain she knew was buried deep in his heart.

She knew how Josh felt about family, knew how he'd feel about his own child, and knew how devastating something like this would be for him.

"I'm so sorry, Josh. So very sorry." She cursed the coldness of a woman who could lie and deceive Josh, then so callously deprive him of something he so desperately wanted.

Em wished she would have been here for Josh, to give him the support and love he'd needed during that time in the same way he'd given them to her since the day she'd come home.

"Not as sorry as I was," he admitted with a sad smile. "She never even gave me a chance, Em. She never even asked if maybe *I* wanted my child. If she didn't want me, fine, I could have lived with that. But why did she have to destroy our child?" Even now, after all these years the pain was still raw and deep. "I never saw or heard from her again."

"You're probably better off without her," Em said, unable to keep the resentment out of her voice. She couldn't imagine anyone just walking away from a man like Josh, and destroying a child they'd created together.

"Definitely," he agreed, reaching for his water glass to take a sip. He shrugged, setting his glass back down. "Up until then, Em, I guarded my heart. You know how I felt after Jesse's kidnapping, and then after my parents were killed."

She nodded, remembering all too well. "You told me once that you would never allow yourself to love anyone again because it made you too vulnerable to hurt." She remembered how hurt she'd been at the time, remembered how much she feared that Josh had locked his heart away forever.

"Exactly. And I meant it." He stared into his glass. "But Melanie, well, she slipped through my defenses, and then deliberately lied to me and betrayed me. I thought she was an honest, honorable woman, someone I would have been proud to have as my wife, as the mother of my children." He shook his head. "I don't know how I could have been so wrong." He lifted his gaze to Em's. "She was the first person, the first woman I allowed myself to trust in many years, Em, and what she did to me—to us, to our child..." His voice trailed off and he shook his head again. "I don't know how I could have been so foolish. How I could have not seen what she was truly like." He'd been too blinded by love, he realized now, knowing he could and would never let that happen to him again. He couldn't risk it. "I've never forgiven myself for not protecting my child."

The tone of his voice made her heart ache for him, and for the child he'd lost. He was the kind of man who would always step up to the plate and take responsibility for his actions.

And knowing how he felt about children, she could only imagine the heartbreak he'd gone through, heartbreak he still carried every day of his life, judging from the look on his face.

"Oh, Josh," she said softly, lifting his hand to kiss it before pressing it to her cheek, needing to touch him right now. "It's not your fault. You're not the one who... It wasn't your decision to—"

"No, Em, but it was *my* child, and I had a responsibility to protect it, to take care of it. And I didn't," he added so sadly that Em's eyes filled with tears again. He looked up at her, his gaze haunted. ‘‘Em, I don’t think I’ll ever be able to forgive myself. Because I mistakenly thought I loved someone, because I trusted her, it cost me my child. I don’t think I could endure…such pain ever again.’’

‘‘Oh, Josh.’’ Em wanted to hug him and hold him until all the pain and hurt and desolation inside him melted. The resentment she felt toward the woman who had so cruelly deceived him knew no bounds. ‘‘I’m so sorry.’’ She held his hand tightly. ‘‘So very sorry.’’

There was nothing else she could say she knew that would ease Josh’s pain or erase his guilt. Nor was there anything she could say that would change his mind about loving. She knew it; had known it since she was twelve and had foolishly professed her love for Josh. The thought that he wouldn’t allow himself to love anyone, to share his life with someone made her infinitely sad.

Dear Josh.

He deserved to have a wonderful woman, a wonderful life, and a wonderful family more than anyone else she knew. He was the kind of man a woman dreamed about, a man who would honor and cherish any woman in his life, and their children.

Now she understood why he was so concerned, so protective about her and Baby Cakes. He hadn’t been able to protect his own child, and so he was determined to make sure he helped her protect hers.

Em’s heart softened, and all the love she’d felt for Josh over the years flowed and flourished through her veins, deepening into something far more than friendship, frightening her.

She wasn’t going to think about that fear now, or

her feelings. Right now, all she wanted—needed—to do was comfort Josh.

"Josh, I guess when we think we're in love, we all make mistakes in judgment. Look at me. I thought for certain Jack was the perfect man, the kind of man who wanted what I wanted."

"And what did you want, Em?" Josh asked carefully.

She smiled, toying with her glass. "That's the easy part, Josh. I wanted what your parents had. It's true," she said when he glanced at her in surprise. She sighed dreamily. "I always thought your parents had a perfect marriage and the perfect family." She sighed again. "I was so envious of all of you," she added with a laugh.

He smiled, his thoughts going back to what his brother Jared had told him this morning about Em eventually falling in love and marrying someone else. Josh had no idea why the idea bothered him so much.

"Well, nothing's perfect, Em, but I have to agree with you. My parents' marriage was pretty near perfect." He could think about his parents now, and talk about them without feeling the gut-wrenching pain he once did. Now, the pain had drifted into very happy memories.

"They were always so loving, so supportive of one another. And so kind," Em said, remembering. "Every time your dad looked at your mom his eyes lit up like a Christmas tree." Embarrassed, she flushed. "That's what I wanted, Josh. A man who felt that way about me."

"That's what every woman deserves, Em," he said with a smile. Then he sobered and asked carefully, "But Jack didn't?"

She shook her head. "He was too busy looking at and chasing other women to even notice me."

Furious, Josh's face darkened and he leaned closer. "I can't believe that man—"

"It's over, Josh," she said with a relieved sigh. "And I can't say that I'm sorry about it." She smiled slowly. "Just sorry it took me so long to realize just what kind of man he was. Or rather wasn't," she added, realizing that Jack couldn't hold a candle to Josh. Not in any area.

"How did you stand it for so long, Em?" Josh asked.

She shrugged. "I kept thinking Jack would change. That eventually he'd grow up and want to settle down." Absently, she ran a finger around the rim of her glass. "When I discovered I was pregnant, well, I thought for sure I'd finally have the husband—the family—I'd always wanted."

"And deserved," Josh added, wondering if Em still wanted all those things.

"But he took off so fast I'm surprised he didn't leave skid marks." She shook her head. "I knew he was lacking in character, but I had no idea he'd do something like that, just simply take off and abandon me and the baby without so much as a backward glance."

His heart ached at the sadness he heard in her voice. "Oh, God, Em, I know pride alone would have prevented you from calling your father, but I still don't understand why you didn't call me. I would have helped you, you know that." Josh hated the fact that she'd been at the mercy of the man she'd married. A man who should have protected her and their unborn child, instead of tossing them away like nothing more than yesterday's newspaper.

"I know," she admitted softly. "But Josh, there'd been so many years, so much water under the bridge." She glanced up at him. "I didn't know—" She shrugged. "I just didn't know what to expect." She didn't want to admit to Josh that she would never have called him simply because she wanted—needed—to finally stand on her own two feet. He'd been around most of her life, picking up the shattered pieces of her heart, her life, her emotions. But she'd been a child then.

Now she was an adult, and she had to handle things on her own.

"So tell me, Em," Josh asked carefully, his gaze never leaving hers. "What do you want now?"

"Now?" Thoughtfully, she turned to look out the window before bringing her gaze back to his. All the yearning and longings she'd had all her life, the need to have a home of our own, a real home, and a family who loved and accepted her came rushing to the surface, smothering her in a wash of aching sadness. She looked at him and tried to smile, but couldn't quite pull it off. The yearning inside was suddenly too strong, too deep, consuming her.

"What I want now, Josh," she said softly. "Is peace. Just some peace, stability and security. I guess I've been looking—searching—for a home my whole life. Well, at least since Mama died," she added. Her voice hitched, then broke. With anyone else she would have been embarrassed, but this was Josh, and she had no reason to be embarrassed. If anyone would understand, he would. Absently, she swiped at her tears, feeling a profound sadness for the lonely little girl she'd been, and the terrified young woman she'd become.

But that was in the past, she realized proudly. She'd done what she needed to do, and would make no apologies to anyone. She'd changed and grown in these months since she'd learned she was about to become a mother. Changed into a self-sufficient, self-reliant, mature adult capable of taking care of herself and her child without anyone else's help. And she couldn't help but feel a profound sense of pride in her accomplishments for the first time in her life.

"I'm going to make a home for myself, Josh, and for my baby." She smiled, but her lips trembled. "A real home, filled with love and laughter, security and stability. My baby is never going to feel unloved or unwanted, nor is she ever going to feel like she's a disappointment to me, the way I always did with Daddy." She had to swallow the lump in her throat. "I'm never going to allow myself to depend on anyone ever again to give me the things I need to be happy." She glanced down at the table, her vision blurred from tears. "I finally learned that you can't expect someone else to love you unless you love yourself." Her smile was thin. "And I'm learning, Josh. And I'm trying to forgive myself for allowing Jack to do to me what he did." There was so much shame over what she'd allowed her husband to do to her in the name of love.

"It wasn't your fault, Em," Josh said softly.

"Yes, it was," she admitted. "It was all my fault. I was so desperate to get away from Daddy, so desperate to have someone truly love me, to feel like I truly belonged somewhere—anywhere—that I didn't look before I leaped. Because I thought I loved Jack, it blinded me to everything else. Loving him made me lose all sense of judgment. I can't ever let that happen again, Josh. I can't ever put myself, or more importantly, my baby at risk like that. Not for a man, not for anyone.'' And she thought sadly, especially not for love.

She swiped her eyes, then swallowed before continuing. ''I never want Baby Cakes to know her father didn't want her, Josh. Not ever. I'm going to love her enough so it won't ever matter that she doesn't have her father around. I'll be both parents to her, anything and everything she needs. And I'm going to love her more than any baby has ever been loved.'' Em touched her belly, closing her eyes and saying a small prayer of thanks for the miracle she'd been given—the miracle of her child.

Josh sat there for a moment, just watching Em, his calm, quiet eyes going over her beautiful features, knowing that at this moment, he'd never felt closer or more connected to anyone.

He thought about Jared's words again and couldn't imagine, couldn't even conceive of any man feeling any closer to Em or her baby. ''Em, do you know what I want?''

''No,'' she said with a smile, resting her chin on her hand. ''I don't. But I imagine you're going to tell me?''

''Em,'' he said slowly. ''What I want is for you to marry me.''

Chapter Nine

Stunned, for long silent moments Em merely stared at Josh, his words reverberating over and over in her mind as her heart fluttered wildly, hopefully inside her chest.

"Josh," she demanded finally, unaware that her voice had risen loud enough to attract the attention of nearby diners. "Are you drunk?"

With a laugh, he held up his empty glass, glancing at the nearby guests who were practically leaning out of their chairs in an effort to hear their conversation. "Not after only one glass of wine, Em."

"Sick, then?" she asked hopefully, reaching across the table to lay a hand to his forehead. If he was sick, even a bit feverish, perhaps that would explain his strange behavior. If he was a bit delusional from fever, *that* would even be better, *that* she could understand. Maybe.

He laughed again, capturing her hand and bringing it to her mouth for a gentle kiss. She refused to acknowledge the fact that her pulse sped up and her blood heated. "No, Em, I'm not sick, either."

Totally shocked and confused, Em shook her head, trying to make some sense out of this. "Josh, I'm sorry, but I don't understand," she admitted, her gaze searching his frantically.

His proposal had come out of the blue, taking her by surprise, stunning her so that she had a hard time thinking, let alone speaking.

She couldn't even begin to comprehend where on earth his question had come from. More importantly, she couldn't begin to fathom why on earth Josh had asked *her* to marry him.

Years ago, she would have given anything to have Josh want to marry him, but that was then. This was now.

Her situation and circumstances were totally, completely different. She was a different person then. And so was he.

Looking at him carefully, she could see the mischief lurking in those glorious blue eyes and her temper begin to simmer. She knew him well enough to know this wasn't a casual question; no, marriage was far too serious and important to Josh Ryan to just foolishly pop it on someone. Even her.

For a Ryan, marriage was a sacred vow, meant to last a lifetime. It wasn't something they took lightly.

So what on earth was Josh up to? she wondered, narrowing her gaze on him as she considered all the possibilities.

He must have planned this, she thought. He must have some plan in mind, otherwise he wouldn't have asked her to marry him. Not serious Josh Ryan who'd vowed never to risk loving anyone ever again.

A dawning thought had her scowl deepening. He was up to something. Again. She just knew it! Something in his determination to protect the poor pregnant single mom who clearly didn't have enough sense to protect herself. The thought had her temper simmering just below the surface.

''What's to understand, Em?'' he asked with a careless shrug of his shoulders, clearly not seeing anything wrong with his out-of-the blue question. He was trying hard not to be offended by her response, but he would have felt better had she been just a little happy about it, instead of acting as if he had just told her he was about to abscond with the contents of her purse.

''Why on earth would you ask me to marry you?'' she demanded.

He shrugged, fingering the rim of his empty wine glass. ''Why not?''

''Oh, my word,'' Em muttered. Just what every woman wanted to hear when a man asked her to marry him! Fearing she might do or say something she'd regret, Em dropped her napkin to the table and yanked her hand free so she could stand up.

''Josh,'' she said, desperately trying to hang on to her temper. ''Would you please take me home?''

''Sure.'' With ease, Josh stood up, pushed in his chair, then took her elbow, guiding her through the restaurant to the elevator that would take them right to the underground garage.

''You know,'' he whispered into her ear as he led her out of the elevator toward his car, making a shiver race the length of her. ''I don't ask a woman to marry me every day of the week.'' He grinned down at her, wondering what she was scowling about.

"Well, I suppose that's something to be thankful for," she snapped. She started going in one direction while he went another. Turning her by her elbow, he took her along with him.

"I mean it's not like you've got to stand in line and take a number like at the butcher," he said, making her come to a halt and glance at him wildly.

"A number?" she repeated. "Like at the butcher? Ugh!" Grinding her teeth, Em continued walking, not certain she was going in the right direction.

"Em."

"What!"

He took her elbow, trying not to laugh. "You're...uh...going the wrong way again. The car's over here." Still holding on to her for fear she'd storm off, he turned her down another aisle, earning a scathing look from her. Deliberately, he slowed his steps to accommodate her shorter legs. He was trying to make light of the situation, but she apparently wasn't interested if that scowl on her face was any indication.

"Even though I don't have much experience at this, Em, it seems to me that when a man asks you to marry him, you're not supposed to get mad at him."

"Mad?" she repeated, trying not to grind her teeth together. Mad wouldn't even begin to cover what she was feeling. "No woman wants to feel as if a man's asking her to marry him simply because marriage is the lesser of two evils. Or a fate worse then death," she added.

"Well, I didn't quite mean to make it come off that way," he admitted.

"Well, you failed," she said, making him laugh. "Miserably."

He stopped to unlock her car door. She stopped with him. "Em?"

"What?" She forced herself to look up at him, then saw those incredible blue eyes and felt that yearning deep in her heart, a yearning that had her knees shaking, annoying her.

"Baby Cakes needs a father," he said softly, making her gaze narrow. So that was it! Now she understood. This had nothing to do with her at all, nothing to do with his feelings for *her,* and everything to do with what he *thought* her baby needed.

Em wanted to scream in frustration. Josh didn't really want to marry *her,* he was asking her out of some misguided sense of duty he felt toward the baby.

She sighed, wishing she could start this evening all over again, wishing it didn't hurt to know Josh had asked her to be his wife, not because he loved her or wanted to be with her, but because he wanted to make sure her baby had a father.

Her emotions tangled, and she was torn between her own hurt pride and heart, and an overwhelming rush of love for him for caring about her child so very much.

But she certainly wasn't about to marry him simply because he thought her baby needed a father.

"Josh," she began carefully, forcing herself to take a deep breath, "plenty of children grow up without a father and do quite well. Studies have shown that single mothers are quite capable of raising happy, healthy children on their own." When she reached for the door handle, he covered her hand to stop her and she sighed, closing her eyes and praying for patience. ''Josh,'' she said, turning to him. ''Baby Cakes *has* a father. That's how I got pregnant in the first place, remember?''

''No,'' he said firmly, placing his hands on either side of the car, basically pinning her in so he could look down into her gorgeous—albeit furious—face. ''Jack is not a father, Em, he was merely a sperm donor. It takes a lot more to make a father, Em. A lot more.'' The moment the words were out, he realized his mistake. Tears flooded her eyes and slipped unheeded down her cheeks as she merely stared at him, absorbing the verbal blow.

''Em, I'm sorry.'' Blowing out a breath, Josh shook his head. This wasn't turning out exactly how he'd planned. ''I didn't mean that quite the way it sounded.''

Sniffling, she took the handkerchief he offered and wiped her eyes. Em took a slow, deep breath, trying to get her emotions under control, not trusting herself to speak until she did.

''It's the truth, Josh,'' she admitted, forcing herself to look at him. ''Jack was little more than...a sperm donor,'' she repeatedly softly, tears shimmering again. ''I can't and won't make excuses for him.'' He didn't deserve anything from her, not excuses, not sympathy and especially not her forgiveness.

Jack had made a conscious choice to walk away from her and their baby. It was his decision to abandon his unborn child. She'd not make excuses for such behavior. Ever. It wasn't her style.

She fully believed you weren't an adult until you accepted responsibility for your actions. She had a feeling she would be an old woman before Jack Bowen ever took responsibility for anything or anyone. Unfortunately, neither she nor the baby had the time to wait. So she'd had to be responsible enough for both of them.

"And you shouldn't have to make excuses for him, Em." Josh touched her face, hating the pain he saw in her eyes, knowing another man had carelessly put that pain there.

Josh's fists clenched impotently and he wished he had Jack Bowen alone for just a few minutes. He imagined the man wouldn't be so brave picking on someone his own size.

"I won't ever excuse his behavior, Josh." She shook her head. "I can't. What he did..." Her voice trailed off. "It's done now, Josh, and I've tried to go on, tried to make the best of a bad situation."

"You have, Em. You've been remarkable," he said. "Not many women would have been able to handle what you handled, and still stand upright and keep going, never letting anything get to them." His gaze caressed her beautiful face and he wondered if she knew how much he admired her, respected her for all that she'd done and been through. His heart simply filled whenever he thought about her, about the kind of woman she was, the kind of mother she'd be.

"Thank you, Josh," she said with a sniffle and a watery smile. "That means a lot coming from you."

"Em, I'm sorry," he whispered, cupping her chin in his hand so she was forced to look at him. "I didn't mean to hurt you." Feeling guilty, Josh just wanted to gather her in his arms and hold her until her tears stopped and her heart stopped aching. He knew her well enough to know she was hurting inside, and doing her best to hide it. And it just made every protective instinct he'd ever have grow and strengthen.

She shrugged, crumbling his hanky in her hand and pushing a tumble of curls off her face. "Sometimes the truth hurts, Josh." She sighed, leaning against the car. She was suddenly so weary, she realized. Just so unbearably weary.

"Em, I want you to think about something. What are you going to tell Baby Cakes when she's old enough to start asking questions? When she wants to know who her father is, and more importantly where he is? And what are you going to say when she asks why her father isn't with her like all the other kid's fathers?"

Wearily, Em shook her head. "I…I don't know Josh," she admitted honestly. "I…I…haven't thought that far ahead." She'd been so concerned with the here and now, so consumed with just surviving day by day, she hadn't really thought that far ahead, hadn't really thought about the future, or life after the baby was born. Nor had she thought about what she would say, what kind of answers she would give when her child was old enough to start asking questions, questions Em knew she might not be able to answer.

How on earth could she tell her precious baby girl that her own father didn't want her? Em swallowed hard against the flush of fresh tears, her heart aching in a way it hadn't since she was a child.

She knew firsthand how it would hurt, knowing your own father didn't love or want you. Hadn't she lived with the pain most of her life from her own father?

Em shook her head, feeling overwhelmed and

slightly panicked. She would never, ever admit such a thing to her child, never deliberately hurt her; and Em knew that the truth would hurt her child, crush her heart and her spirit and make her feel as if there was something inherently wrong with *her* that her own father didn't love or want her.

How could she do that to her own precious baby?

She couldn't, Em realized. No matter what, she would never, ever tell her daughter about Jack or his actions. Not ever.

Not to protect Jack; he deserved no protection. But to protect Baby Cakes.

Em sighed wearily, lifting a hand to rub her temple where a tension headache had started. She honestly thought she could do this herself. Honestly thought she had a handle on things. That she could love the baby enough so that her child wouldn't miss having a father. Now, she wasn't so sure and it scared the daylights out of her.

"Em, look, I know you probably haven't had much time to give any thought to the future and what you'll tell Baby Cakes when she's old enough to start asking questions. But Em I have, and Baby Cakes needs—deserves—a father. Every kid does. Baby Cakes deserves a father who loves her, cares about her, who is there for her and spends time with her." Josh took a deep breath. "Baby Cakes needs me, Em," he finished softly. "I love her already."

"Oh, Josh." She wasn't going to cry. She simply wasn't, but she did. A soft sob escaped her and she gave in to it, letting Josh pull her into his arms to hug her tight.

"Don't cry, Em," he whispered, tenderly stroking her back, savoring the warmth and feel of her.

"I'm not crying," she insisted with a sniffle.

"Yes, I can see that you're not crying," he teased, leaning back to look at her.

She glanced up at him, saw all the things she'd never expected. Love. Concern. Caring. She wanted to cry harder. How could he care so much for her precious baby when Baby Cakes's own father didn't care one whit about her?

If Em wasn't already in love with Josh, she realized with a soggy sigh, after tonight she would have been.

And there was no point in denying it. But because she *knew* she was in love with him, she wasn't going to marry him.

She simply couldn't. It wouldn't be fair to Josh, who deserved more than a marriage for convenience's sake.

He didn't love *her*, she reminded herself, ignoring the searing pain in her heart. And he deserved to have a wife he loved, not one who was just a friend.

His marriage proposal was kind, extremely generous and exactly want she would have expected from a man like Josh.

Dear Josh, she thought, her heart aching.

"Josh." With great deliberation, Em took a slow, deep breath, then drew back to look at him. "I'm honored and touched by your proposal. Honestly," she added when his brows knit.

"But you're not going to marry me?" he said dismally, wondering why it hurt so much.

"No, I'm not," she said, laying a hand to his chest. "I can't even begin to tell you how much it means to me to know that you love Baby Cakes and want to be her father. It touches me in a way nothing has in a long, long time. But Josh, marrying you to give

Baby Cakes a father simply wouldn't be fair to you. You deserve more than a marriage of convenience."

"But Em—"

"Josh, you'll always be a part of Baby Cakes's life as a trusted friend, a confidant, maybe even her first crush," she added with a twinkle in her eye.

"Why, Em? Just tell me why?" He covered her hand with his, joining his fingers with hers, wanting to join their hearts in the same way. He didn't think of this as a marriage of convenience, he thought it would be a marriage...of the heart. Another thought had him nearly panicking. "Don't you think I'd be a good father?"

She laughed simply because the idea was so absurd. "Someday, when you find a woman you love and truly want and should marry, I have no doubt that you're going to be a fabulous father."

"But you don't want me to be the father of *your* child, is that it?"

Em couldn't bear to see the hurt in his eyes. It would be easier to talk to him if he didn't have his arms around her, if she couldn't feel his warmth or his protection.

"Josh, do you remember earlier tonight in the restaurant when you asked me what I wanted now?"

"Yeah," he said, not certain where she was going with this.

"I told you what I wanted now was a real home, filled with love and laughter, security and stability." She had to swallow the lump in her throat. "Josh, if I marry you, it will be simply to give Baby Cakes a father, and that's not a real good basis for a marriage." She hesitated, wanting him to understand. "I had a marriage in name only before, a marriage where my husband didn't love me.'' She shook her head. ''I have no intention of ever having that kind of marriage again. It wouldn't be good for me, nor would it be good for the baby.'' She took a deep breath, then squared her shoulders. ''Josh, if I ever get married again, I want the fairy tale,'' she admitted with the shrug. ''The *real* fairy tale this time, Josh. Not the imitation. I want it all, Josh. The love, the caring, the tenderness, the understanding. A true partner. I want a marriage that will give both me and Baby Cakes a real home and a family, the kind I've always wanted and dreamed about. And I want a man that I can love with all my heart, knowing he'll love me as much in return.''

''But Em, you know I care about you,'' he protested, trying to make sense out of his own feelings. He cared for her. More than he could put into words. Much more than he'd ever realized until tonight when he'd asked her to marry him, when he thought about spending his life with her, every day, every night, together.

He hadn't realized how much he'd been thinking about spending his life with her until she'd turned down his marriage proposal.

''Of course you do, Josh, and I care about you.'' *I love you,* she thought, but because she did love him she wouldn't cheat him out of a chance to be with a woman he really loved and wanted to marry for all the right reasons. ''Too much to accept your proposal. But I thank you, Josh. Thank you for being the most wonderful, kind, caring friend a woman could ever have.'' She leaned up and kissed him on the cheek. ''Let's go home, now,'' she said, and he nodded, opening the door for her with an irritated scowl, then sliding behind the wheel and starting the car.

Em only thought of him as a friend.

He glanced at her, and felt something deep and profound stir inside him, and he wondered when he'd started thinking of Em as *more* than a friend.

Much more.

He wasn't sure. All he knew at the moment, was that he'd just blown it.

"You set one foot on that ladder, Em and I'm telling Josh." Jake wiped his hands on his glue-splattered rag, stepped closer to the ladder he'd just come down off of, then laughed at the smoldering look she shot him.

"Tattletale," she complained, trying to hide a grin. "I just want to see how the ceiling looks. Up close." She glanced up at the ceiling where Jake had just finished putting up oak crown molding.

She glanced around the master bedroom, then hugged herself, pleased. Everything in the house was finally coming together. Jake, Jared and Josh had spent the weekend painting, plastering and wallpapering.

The master bedroom which had once been dark and depressing, now was awash in shades of pale green and pink. The upper walls had been wallpapered in a small rose-striped print, then Jake had added an oak chair rail to separate the wall, finishing them off by painting the bottom a pale green, picking up the same color in the wallpaper. She'd already chosen a matching green-and-pink quilt and curtains, and now she couldn't wait to get everything put together. With only a few weeks until her due date, she was anxious to have everything finished.

"It's beautiful, Jake," Em confessed, twirling around in delight. The house was finally beginning to look and feel like a real home.

"Should be," Jake complained good-naturedly, chugging down a full glass of lemonade and wiping his brow. "I've had lots of practice." He rolled his eyes. "Rebecca's had me doing the same thing at our place."

"How's she feeling?" Em asked, taking his glass and refilling it from the pitcher sitting on the drop-cloth-covered floor. "I imagine this heat is unbearable for her now."

"She's churlish," Jake admitted with another grin, flashing the dimple the Ryan men were known for. "But tell her I said that and I'll lie and deny it."

Em laughed. "She's only got another week or so to go so I imagine she's entitled."

"You're right," he admitted, swiping his brow again. "But I'll be happy once the baby comes. Finally." Pride and love shone in his face.

"Goofing off again, bro?" Jared walked into the bedroom, dressed similarly in paint-splattered shirt and cutoffs. He glanced around, surveying his brother's handiwork. "Not bad," he said, walking around in a circle and giving a nod of approval. "Not bad at all."

"Thanks," Jake said sarcastically. "Nice of you to approve."

"Josh needs us in the nursery," Jared said, reaching for his brother's glass of lemonade and draining it in one sip.

"Can I come, too?" Em asked with a mischievous

smile. Josh had banned her from the nursery from the moment he'd finished prepping the walls. As a baby gift for Baby Cakes he'd insisted on decorating the entire room, but wouldn't let Em see it until it was totally done. And she was so antsy and curious, she could just spit.

"No!" Jake and Jared caroled in unison. "Josh will have our heads." Jared draped an arm around Em's shoulders. "Just be patient, Em. He'll let you see it as soon as he's finished."

"But—"

"Em, the way I hear it, he'll be finished before dark falls tomorrow night—"

"Tomorrow?" she asked in excitement, earning a nod from Jared.

"Yep." He glanced at his brother. "Providing he gets some help," Jared said meaningfully. They both knew Josh was hurrying to finish the house because Em's baby shower was tomorrow.

Jake shrugged, pocketing his rag. "You know those lawyer types, all thumbs when it comes to *real* work." He wiggled his brows at Em. "Come on, bro, let's go help the guy out."

"Can I do anything to help?" Em called, following Jake and Jared down the hallway, sidestepping the ladder Josh had left propped against the wall and hoping for a peek at the nursery.

"Yeah, make some more lemonade," Jake requested with a grin before slipping inside the nursery with his brother and shutting the door firmly behind him.

For a moment, Em stood there, listening to the brothers talk, laugh and joke with one another. They sounded like just what they were, she thought with a smile. A family. A real family. They were close, loving and always a part of each other's lives. One always knew they could count on the other for anything and everything.

They'd always had that luxury, she thought wistfully. Always had the benefit of knowing they belonged. Something she'd never once felt in her life.

Something her own child would feel.

She'd make certain of it.

With a wistful sigh of yearning, Em turned and headed back down the hall.

Em looked so peaceful sleeping on the couch that Josh hated to wake her up. But it was late, way past the dinner hour and he knew she hadn't eaten yet. After helping him clean up, his brothers had gone home, and Josh had taken the time to shower and change before deciding to wake her.

"Em?" Gently, Josh sat next to her on the couch and touched her shoulder. "Em, hon, it's time to wake up." He touched her shoulder again, then watched her slowly awaken. Her eyes fluttered several times. She scrubbed at her nose, then pushed her hair sleepily off her face, making him smile.

"Josh?" Her voice was groggy with sleep. Her eyes fluttered again and then she smiled that beautiful, glorious smile. "What time is it?" she asked, slightly befuddled as she glanced toward the window and saw night had fallen.

"Almost eight."

"Morning or night?"

He laughed. "Night. It's still Saturday night, Em." Tenderly, he tucked a strand of hair behind her ear and helped her to sit up. ''I wouldn't have woken you but I figured you must be getting hungry by now.''

''You have paint in your hair,'' she said, lifting a finger to touch the area where several strands on the side of his head were clumped together by a particularly brilliant shade of pink.

''I'm surprised my whole head's not painted,'' he admitted, rubbing his skinned knuckles. Although he and his brothers had always done manual labor around the ranch while they were growing up, it had been a long, long time since he'd actually physically exerted himself the way he had the past few weeks getting Em's house ready for the baby.

''Are you hungry?'' he asked and she nodded, rubbing her belly.

''Starving.''

''It's too hot to cook, Em, so I ordered some ribs from Rico's in town.'' He glanced at his watch. ''I've got to pick them up in about ten minutes. That sound okay?''

''Ribs?'' Her face brightened and she fairly swooned. ''I've had such a taste for ribs the past couple of days— What?'' she asked abruptly when he started to laugh. ''What are you laughing about Joshua Ryan?''

''You've mentioned it, ah...more than a few times.'' He stroked a finger down her cheek. She looked so soft and beautiful, her skin glowing, her eyes gleaming.

She laughed, rubbing her belly again. ''Can't help it. It seems like I'm starving all the time now. Heat or not.''

His brows knit and he glanced down. She was rubbing her belly again in a way that let him know the baby was rambunctious. ''Baby Cakes getting restless again?''

She nodded, stifling a yawn. ''She's been kicking up a storm all day, and I think she has the hiccups. Again,'' she admitted with a laugh.

''Here, let me.'' Josh began slowly massaging Em's belly, cooing softly to the baby.

''You're going to spoil her, Josh,'' Em whispered, unable to resist laying a hand to the silk of his hair. Her eyes slid closed as he continued to soothe and comfort Baby Cakes, to whisper soft, sweet, nonsensical words to her.

''That's what babies are for, Em, to spoil.'' He lifted his head and their eyes met and held for a long silent moment. Unable to resist, desperately wanting—needing—to feel connected to him, she laid her hand over his.

''Josh, you are going to make a wonderful father some day,'' she said quietly, feeling a rush of love for him and for her baby nearly overfill her heart.

Josh was such a kind, wonderful man with the capacity to love in a way she'd never known any other man to be. It touched her so deeply, and made the yearning inside her grow day by day. ''You know that?'' She couldn't bear to think about Josh married—to someone else—doing all these wonderful, loving things. Since the night he'd asked her to marry her, Em had not been able to stop thinking about the fact that one day Josh would marry someone else.

The thought of it almost broke her heart.

Immediately Em regretted her thoughts, knowing she was being selfish. If anyone deserved the fairy tale, a loving wife and a loving family, it was Josh.

Still, she couldn't stop the twinge of jealousy that touched her heart.

"Seems like she's settling down," he said softly, slowly caressing Em's belly and watching her face go soft and dreamy at his touch. "I think she's falling asleep," he said, smiling at Em. Whenever she looked like this, so vulnerable, so fragile, it took all his self-control not to just scoop her up into his arms and hold her close, to protect her and Baby Cakes from anything and everything that could ever hurt them.

He treasured the peaceful pleasure he saw in her eyes, on her face every day. Treasured it and wanted to make sure it stayed there.

Em smiled, then lay her head back on the couch, feeling sleepy and contented. "I think so, Josh. You know, it's almost like she knows it's you rubbing my belly. When I do it, all she does is kick and fuss some more, but when you do it, well, it's as if the moment she hears your voice, feels your touch she seems to calm right down." Sort of like her mother, Em thought wistfully, realizing just what a calming effect Josh had had on her life since she'd come home. And still marveling at it.

Standing, he grinned down at her. "Kid's got good taste, what can I tell you?" He glanced at his watch. "I'm going to run into town to pick up our food. Can I get you anything while I'm there? More ice cream? Lemonade? Anything?"

She shook her head. "No, thanks, Josh. I think I've got everything I need."

Dipping his hands in his pockets to search for his keys, Josh headed toward the door. "Oh, Em, there's an unopened overnight letter on the table over there. I didn't know if you'd seen it or not, so I thought I'd better mention it.'' He glanced at the table before pushing the screen door open. ''It's next to the phone,'' he said, letting the door slam shut behind him.

''Good Lord,'' Em muttered. ''I completely forgot about it. It was delivered last week, the night we had dinner.''

''Oh and Em?''

She glanced up at him through the screen door. ''Yes?''

''Stay out of the nursery,'' Josh said.

''Spoilsport,'' she called with a laugh, watching Josh take the stairs two at a time.

With a yawn and a huge stretch, Em got up slowly, easing her cramped legs, wondering who on earth would send her an overnight letter.

Only one way to find out, she thought, crossing the room to pick up the letter. With a frown, she tore open the envelope and read it quickly. Before the entire letter registered, her head began to spin and she feared her knees would buckle.

Taking a slow, deep breath, she knew she'd better sit down. Em went to the couch, then slowly let herself sink back down into the cushions, reading the letter again, letting each and every typewritten word sink in before carefully folding the letter back up and replacing it in the envelope once again.

She should have known that once Jack was found, he'd figure out she'd come home to Saddle Falls. Where else would she go? He knew she had no other family, no other place to go. But apparently he didn't know her father had passed away months ago.

Nor, apparently did he know that she was no longer his wife.

Letting her eyes slide closed, Em leaned her head back against the couch. She should have figured that. Jack had been AWOL when her divorce had been granted on the grounds of desertion. It wasn't like she had an address to send him the notice. No wonder Jack believed they were still married, believed he was still about to become a father. Em's eyes darkened.

Had no idea that he was no longer welcome in her life. Or her baby's.

The *baby*, Em thought, placing a hand on her belly and fighting a bout of panic. Baby Cakes was *her* baby. Not Jack's. Like Josh had said, Jack was little more than a sperm donor, and it took more than that to become a father. A lot more. Josh had been more of a father, a real father to Baby Cakes during her pregnancy than Jack was even capable of.

"Don't you worry, Baby Cakes," Em said in an oddly quiet voice, placing a protective hand over her belly. "Jack may be back, but he's *not* your daddy. No matter what he says or thinks," she added firmly, letting her eyes slide closed, and wondering what on earth she was going to do.

One thing *was* certain. She was not going to let Jack Bowen into her life or her child's ever again.

Chapter Ten

"Em," Josh said nervously, trying to bank his impatience. "Could you hurry up here? I promised the fire chief we'd meet him at the diner at two." He glanced at his watch, knowing Rebecca and Natalie would have his hide if he didn't get Em to the diner pretty soon. They were almost a half an hour late as it was. Em was going to be the only woman who missed her own baby shower he thought with a scowl. "Em?"

"Josh, I'm coming," she said with a sigh, moving slowly down the hall toward him. "I'm too big to be moving any faster than this," she complained, grabbing her sweater off the chair. "And why on earth the fire chief decided he wanted to inspect the diner today on Sunday when the diner is closed is beyond me."

"It's because the diner is closed that he wants to do the inspection," Josh lied, taking her elbow and trying to move her along. His brothers were waiting for them to leave in order to deliver and set up the nursery furniture so it would be waiting for Em when they returned. "You don't really want him checking the fire alarms and the sprinklers while you've got a diner full of customers do you?" Josh asked.

She grinned as he opened the front door and helped her down the stairs. "Well, it could be interesting," she said. "Can you just imagine how much excitement that would cause? I'd be the talk of the town, not that I haven't been already," she added with a frown, laying a hand on her belly. Other than Josh and his family and her staff, she hadn't told anyone about the circumstances of her pregnancy. Nor had she told anyone about Jack, or why she'd come home and stayed home. And she knew that had caused more than a few tongues to wag. Not that it bothered her.

"Josh?" She turned to him as he opened the car door for her. A few more weeks, a few more pounds and she wouldn't be able to fit in the front seat.

"What?" He helped her into the seat, waiting until he was certain she was comfortable before handing her the seat belt, and shutting the door.

She waited until he'd slipped behind the wheel and started the car before continuing. "What happens if the fire chief finds code violations? I mean, do I get a chance to fix them? Do I get fined?"

Josh shook his head. He hated lying to her, but he soothed himself with the knowledge that it was for a good cause. And besides, if he didn't, his sisters-in-laws would strangle him.

"I'm not sure, Em," Josh said, taking the back way to the diner so she wouldn't see all the cars that would no doubt be parked in front. "He might close the diner down for a few weeks," he said absently, while searching for a parking space.

"Close me down!" Em cried with a scowl. And Josh knew immediately it was the wrong thing to say. He was just trying to make conversation, just trying to keep her occupied, but he hated all this subterfuge, had no experience at it and judging from the look on her face, he sure wasn't any good at it.

"Come on, Em," he said pulling into a parking space behind the diner and shutting off the car. "Let's go see if he's here."

"But Josh..." Her words trailed off when he shut the door to come around and get her. "Josh," she began again, the moment she was out of the car. "He's going to have to be reasonable."

"Yes, Em, I'm sure he will be," Josh said with a frown, leading her around to the front door of the diner and trying to hold up his end of this conversation.

"I mean, I can't afford to close down, not even for a few days, let alone a few weeks."

"Yes, Em," he repeated dutifully, taking a deep breath. "I know that." He glanced at her once, saw the concern on her face, then unlocked the front to the diner. "Go on in, Em," he said, pocketing the key and taking a step back. This was her day, he thought with a grin. All hers. And more than anything else he wanted her to enjoy it.

"Sur...prise!" The loud chorus of voices had Em taking a step back in stunned surprise.

"J-Josh?"

"I'm right behind you, hon," he said, slipping an arm around her simply because she looked so startled, he feared she might faint. "Go on in, hon," he encouraged, giving her a gentle nudge to get her feet moving.

Wide-eyed, Em clung to Josh for support as her gaze went around the crowded room. Every booth, every table, and even the counter was full. If she wasn't mistaken every woman in town had gathered here.

"Oh, Josh." Tears filled her eyes and Em started to laugh, turning to him. "You knew, Joshua?" she accused, feeling delighted and nearly overwhelmed by emotion. "You knew and didn't tell me?"

"Not me," he said in defense, raising his hands in the air. "I'm no fool. Rebecca and Natalie would have had my head."

"That's right," Natalie said, moving through the crowd to take Em by the arm. "We warned him—"

"We warned all the Ryan men," Rebecca, Jake's wife finished, taking Em's other arm with a smile. She was due—actually overdue right now, and could barely walk. "If any one of them slipped they'd be…grounded, and confined to their rooms until they were too old to say another word." Rebecca grinned at Josh. "Right, bro?"

"I'm not going to argue with a pregnant lady," Josh said, in his own defense.

"Well, that's a switch," Em said over her shoulder, smiling broadly at him as Rebecca and Natalie led her to the guest of honor's table in the middle of the diner. "You're always arguing with me."

Em's hand went to her mouth when she got to the center of the diner. One of the larger tables for four had been decorated with pastel-colored streamers in various shades of pink and blue. The table itself was covered with an assortment of various-size gaily wrapped packages, each one more festive than the next.

On the counter, a complete buffet luncheon had been laid out, and behind the counter stood Agnes, who was grinning broadly.

"Agnes," Em said with a grin, swiping at her tears as she went to give her a hug. "How... When..." Still overwhelmed, Em shook her head. "How on earth did you manage to do all this without me knowing?"

"Well, hon, if the truth be told, I didn't do it myself." She glanced toward the kitchen door. "Ernie and Sammy pitched in. So did Ms. Wilson from the library, Ms. Powers from the drugstore, and even Mrs. O'Connor helped out a bit. We been working all weekend getting the food ready."

"Thanks, Agnes." Em squeezed her hand, feeling surrounded by love. She made her way slowly around the room, saying hello to everyone.

"Em?" Natalie called, pulling out a chair. "Come sit down, now." She stood behind the chair, then glanced at Josh. "She shouldn't be on her feet too long, Josh," Natalie whispered with a knowing lift of her brow.

Josh nodded, then went to Em, steering her gently toward the center of the diner and her chair. "Have a seat, Em," he said, helping her into it whether she wanted to sit or not. "Do you need to take your shoes off?" he asked with a frown, making her smile.

The past week, her feet had been swelling so badly once she got her shoes on, she had a hard time getting them off, so she'd taken to wearing open-toed sandals that she could just slip on and off. But today, because she thought she had a business appointment with the fire chief, she'd worn regular shoes.

"Please?" she said when Josh produced her toeless

sandals from somewhere behind his back. He bent and gently removed her shoes, giving her very sore and swollen feet a brief massage, making her sigh in relief. Then he gently lifted her feet to slip her sandals on. "Thanks, Josh."

"Well," he glanced around at all the women, feeling just a tad out of place. "If you don't need me for anything else, I think I'll leave."

She extended her hand to her. "Josh, would you mind staying?" He'd been through almost every single stage of her pregnancy with her; it was only fair that he be here for this, too.

"Let's open presents, first," Rebecca said with a grin, eliciting a round of applause from the assembled group. With a precision worthy of a military general, Rebecca, Natalie and Agnes set up an assembly line, passing the gaily wrapped presents through it. Natalie unwrapped the presents, then passed it to Rebecca, who jotted down who the present was from while Agnes jotted down what the present was before passing it to Em. With each and every present the oohs and ahhs grew louder and louder.

"Oh, Josh, look," Em said, holding up a sleeper set in a beautiful shade of pink. "Isn't this gorgeous?"

"It's so tiny," he muttered, staring at the garment in horror and reconsidering whether or not he was really up to be a birthing coach.

Halfway through the gift opening, someone passed Em a glass of pink punch. Thirsty, she began to gulp it down. She glanced up because the room seemed to have gone quiet. The guests, who had crowded around to see the gifts, had separated right down the middle allowing for a newcomer to enter.

The man stood not two feet away from her, a charming smile on his handsome face. The plastic glass slipped from her lips.

"Jack." The word slipped out of her and Em jumped to her feet, sinking right back down when her knees nearly buckled. "Jack," she whispered again, so stunned she couldn't speak.

"Hi, Em." His glance went to Josh, who was standing behind Em, his hand protectively on her chair. "I guess...I'm a little...late," he said with a careless smile and a shrug.

Josh took a step closer, fists clenched, his eyes dark. "That would be the understatement of the year."

"Josh, please?"

Em's plea stopped him.

"What are you doing here, Jack?" Em asked quietly, aware that everyone was watching her.

"That's my baby you're carrying. Where else would I be?"

His baby?

Josh glanced at Jack, and realized no matter how he personally felt, no matter the circumstances, Jack Bowen was in fact Baby Cakes's father.

The reality seemed to drive a sharp-pitched stake through Josh's heart. Until this moment, he hadn't known how much he'd come to love Em and the baby, or how much he'd come to think of Baby Cakes as his.

His baby.

At the thought of Baby Cakes, Josh's heart began to ache, knowing that he'd had no right to allow himself to think of her as his, to fall in love with her or to want her.

Baby Cakes wasn't his.

He'd gone through this before, he thought. He'd already lost one baby. He was absolutely certain he couldn't stand around and lose yet another one.

With his heart breaking, Josh knew he couldn't stay there so he turned on his heel, shaking off Rebecca's arm as she tried to stop him.

"Josh. Wait."

He ignored her and went through the kitchen and out the back door of the diner.

Blindly, he got in his car, trying not to think about what was happening back at the diner. He knew how Em felt about Jack, or at least he thought he knew. But then he remembered, too, how Em had felt about family. About her child. About the fairy tale.

And nothing could change the reality: Josh was not Baby Cakes's father. Jack Bowen was and always would be.

However, the man didn't deserve either of them, Josh thought, turning blindly down another street, then realizing too late he was in front of Em's house.

He drove past, not wanting to pull in the driveway, fearing he would see Jack Bowen acting the part of husband and father. With a sigh, Josh shook his head. Jack Bowen didn't deserve Em or the baby.

Where had Jack Bowen been during all these months?

Where had Jack been when Em struggled daily to keep her spirits up, to keep the diner going and everything in her life together?

Where had he been when she sweated and worked through Lamaze class, learning all the things she needed to know in order to bring Baby Cakes safely into the world?

Josh didn't know, but he knew one thing.

He was the one who had been there for Em. *He* was the one who had grown to love Baby Cakes and Em, the way they both deserved to be loved—with his whole heart, his whole soul.

He loved Baby Cakes. And he loved Em.

The thought, the knowledge came out of nowhere, stunning Josh. He had to pull over to the curb when he realized he was driving down the wrong side of the street.

Dragging a hand through his hair, he realized he needed to think. No, he thought, he didn't need to think. He remembered what his grandfather Tommy had once told him about listening to his heart. Well, Josh was listening to his heart now and knew for certain exactly what his heart was telling him.

"Damn," he muttered, making a U-turn in the middle of the street and heading back toward Em's house. He roared up the driveway, then jumped out of the car before it had stopped rocking.

The door was closed, but instead of using his key, he merely lifted his fist and banged on it.

"Em," he called. "Open up, it's me, Josh." He banged harder. "Em, come on open up."

"Josh? Just a minute, let me get my robe on." Hastily tying her sash around her, Em pulled open the door.

"I have to talk to you," he said, pushing past her and not giving her a chance to speak. His gaze took in the entire room. "Where is he?" he demanded, whirling on her.

Em frowned, wondering what on earth was wrong with him. "Who?"

"Jack." Josh stormed around the room, yanking open closet doors.

Em tried not to goggle at Josh, but it was hard. This was calm, stable, responsible Josh? Right now, her reliable, calm, sensible Josh was behaving like a raving lunatic. And she was thrilled. If she didn't know better, she'd swear he was jealous. And nothing could have pleased her more.

"Would you like to look in the laundry hamper, Josh?" she asked sweetly, making him stop and growl something under his breath. Stifling a laugh, she shrugged. "Hey, I was just trying to be helpful."

"If you want to be helpful, Em, you can just tell me where Baby Cakes's father is?" he all but growled at her again.

"Baby Cakes's father?" she said in confusion, trying not to frown at Josh. "Jack? You mean Jack?"

She'd had enough. She went after him, grabbing him by the back of his shirt and turning him around to stop his rampaging through the house.

"Joshua Ryan, are you deaf?" she asked, raising her voice just to make a point. She stood on tiptoe and spoke directly into his startled, and very angry face. "I told you before, or rather you told me, Jack Bowen is *not* Baby Cakes's father. He was merely a sperm donor, remember?" She laid a hand on his shirt. "Josh, listen to me. Is that why you left the diner? Because you thought Jack had come back to claim Baby Cakes?"

"Well, didn't he?" Josh asked, wondering if the man had come back to claim Em as well.

"Yes," she admitted, grabbing onto the front of Josh's shirt so he couldn't start storming around again. "He did." She took a deep breath. "But you can't really believe I'd let him? Accept him back into my life and the baby's after what he did to me?''

''Well—''

''Josh Ryan, I'm surprised at you.'' She gave him a poke in the chest. ''You know me better than that. Do you honestly think I could just forgive and forget that the man is completely lacking in morals, character, and every other attribute required to be a husband and a father?''

Confused, Josh stood there looking down at her. ''I don't know, Em,'' he admitted honestly, wanting to haul her close and into his arms, to protect her from anything that would ever dare to hurt her. Or Baby Cakes.

''Josh, it takes a lot more than being a sperm donor to be a father. It takes love, care and kindness. It takes putting your child ahead of yourself, making their needs, wishes and desires first in your life.'' She took a deep breath, rubbing her belly and praying the pain she was feeling was just another Braxton-Hicks contraction because she had a feeling this would *not* be a good time for Baby Cakes to make an appearance. ''It takes more to be a father, Josh. A lot more. What it takes, Josh, is what you've been to me and to Baby Cakes all these months.'' She laid a hand to his chest, overwhelmed with love for him. ''Josh, you asked me where Baby Cakes's father is. Well...'' Her voice trailed off and she tugged his hand, dragging him to the mirror on the wall in the foyer. ''See that gorgeous guy there,'' she said, grinning as she pointed to his frowning image. ''There's Baby Cakes's father, Josh,'' she said softly, her voice catching as he turned to her. ''You've been her father from the moment you found out about her, Josh.'' Em sniffled, pressing a hand to her back, hoping these pains weren't serious. "Her *real* father," she added softly, glancing up at him, her gaze soft with love. "Josh, you are exactly the kind of father every woman—*any* woman—could want for her child. The kind of father any child could be proud of."

"Em—"

"Josh, I don't know if you're ready to hear this or not," she said, biting her lip partly in pain, partly because of nerves. "But Josh, I—I—love you, and not as a friend, but as so much more. And so does Baby Cakes," she admitted. "You've been everything to me during all these months, Josh, showering me and the baby with love, kindness, attention and affection. You've always put our needs ahead of your own, even when it made me mad." Tears glistened. "That's what a father is, Josh. That's what a true partner is, as well. Like it or not, Josh, *you* are Baby Cakes's daddy, and—" she added, pressing a hand to her back again "—you're the man I want to spend my life with. The man I want a family and the fairy tale with. The only man," she added as his gaze filled with love.

"Oh, Em." He grabbed her, held her close, his heart overflowing with relief, with love, for her, and for the baby. "I love you, Em," he admitted with a long, relieved sigh. "I'm totally, completely in love with you *and* Baby Cakes." He drew back to lay a hand to her cheek, praying this time he'd do this right. "Em," he began slowly. "I—I love you and want to marry you, and have a family with you. I want to make a home with you. I want the whole fairy tale we've both always wanted—needed. And not just because of Baby Cakes or because she needs a father, but because I need both of you, Em. Please, say you'll marry me?''

Her heart leaped. ''Oh Josh.'' She lifted a hand to his cheek. ''I love you, too. And yes I'll—'' she laughed, then lifted his hand to her belly. ''We'll marry you.''

''Oh, Em.'' He drew her close for a kiss that sealed their love, their future.

''Uh...Josh?'' she whispered against his lips. ''Uh, I think you'd better get my suitcase.'' She had to stop to catch her breath as another sharp pain cut through her. ''And the car.''

''Em?'' Confused he drew back and looked at her then went pale as the moon. ''Oh, my God. The baby? Baby Cakes is coming? *Now?*''

She laughed. ''Yes, Josh. Now.'' She inhaled deeply again. ''Right *now.*''

''Okay, stay calm, Em,'' he said, making her laugh when he left her standing there to dash into her bedroom, grabbing a suitcase with each hand. ''Don't worry, Em,'' he said as he hurried toward the door. ''Everything's going to be fine. I'll call Doc Haggerty. No, I'd better get you to the hospital first.'' He darted out the door, threw the suitcases in the trunk, then jumped in the car, started it and roared down the driveway.

Em sat down on the couch, figuring he'd remember he'd forgotten something—sooner or later.

It was sooner.

The door flew open again and he stood there, grinning, looking sheepish and more adorable than she'd ever seen him.

''Sorry, hon.'' He darted across the room to help her to her feet. ''Don't worry, Em, everything's going to be fine.''

"I know, Josh." She grinned up at him. "Finally, I know everything is truly going to be fine." As she walked out of her house, Em turned and glanced at it, realizing that now, with Baby Cakes and Josh, and all the love they had to share, this house was no longer just a house, but finally, it had truly become her home.

The home she'd always wanted.

"I love you, Josh," she said as he helped her into the car.

He bent to kiss her. His hands were shaking so bad he wasn't certain he could drive. "And I love you, too, Em." For an instant he pressed his brow to hers. "And we're going to be a family, Em, just like we've both always wanted, just like we've always dreamed of." He kissed her again. "I love you, Em." Grinning, he shut the door, then hurried around to the driver's side. "Now, let's go meet our daughter!"

Epilogue

Four months later, on a warm sunny day Em and Josh were married under a gorgeous flower canopy in the Ryan family garden with the entire family present.

Rebecca, who had given birth to a baby girl just days after Em, and Natalie were her attendants, and Jake, Jared, and Sammy were Josh's grooms. Josh's grandfather Tommy, beaming with pride and carrying Em and Josh's two-week-old daughter Brie, who'd been named after his late, beloved wife Sabrina, walked Em down the aisle to meet her beaming groom.

"You know, lass," Tommy whispered to Em as he juggled Brie to keep her quiet. "It's a fine, fine day for a wedding." He glanced at her. "And you make a beautiful bride. Your father, he would have been so proud of you."

"Thank you, Tommy," Em whispered, trying to hold back tears. "That means a lot to me."

"Aye, I know, lass, and it's the truth," he insisted,

just in case she doubted. "I'd not lie in front of the Ryan family priest now, would I?"

She grinned. "Nope, not you, Tommy."

"And he would have been so proud of this wee one, so proud," Tommy said, glancing at the baby. "As am I, lass. As am I."

"I hope so, Tommy," she whispered, praying it was true. She'd finally come to peace about her father, finally come to understand that he simply hadn't the words, or hadn't been able to cope with a frightened little girl when his own grief was so strong. With understanding came forgiveness.

"Here you go, lad," Tommy said to Josh as he handed Em over to her groom. "I'll keep the wee one," he said, making the assembled guests chuckle.

"Thanks, Tommy." Beaming, Josh took Emma's hand, and together they turned to face the priest, anxious to say their vows, to pledge their love, forever and eternity.

"Now, lass, what's the problem?" Tommy whispered as Brie began to fuss. "Are you hungry, is that it, lass?" He rocked her, hoping not to disrupt the vows. "Come on, now, lass, you and me, we'll slip into the house and see if we can't find something to put in your belly." Using his cane to steady himself, Tommy gingerly moved back down the aisle and out into the expanse of the garden, cooing softly in Gaelic to Brie.

As he got closer to the house, he could hear the phone ringing and sighed. "Ah, lass, it's another salesmen for sure, trying to sell me something I don't need." He pushed open the sliding glass door, holding the baby carefully. "But alas, I'm a softie and I'll buy whatever's he selling because I remember what it was like to be young and starting out, trying to make my mark in the world.''

Tommy set Brie down in the ancient cradle that Mrs. O'Connor had given to Em as a shower present and reached for the phone.

''Aye, good day to you, this is the Ryan residence.'' Tommy listened for a moment, then gripped the kitchen counter as his knees buckled. ''Jesse,'' he whispered, clutching the receiver and the counter so tightly his knuckles whitened. ''Is it true?'' he whispered, tears streaming down his face. ''Dear God in Heaven, Jesse, my boy, is it really you?''

* * * * *